GLIMMER TRAIN STORIES

PUBLISHED QUARTERLY
in February, May, August, and November by
Glimmer Train Press, Inc.
812 SW Washington Street, Suite 1205
Portland, Oregon 97205-3216 U.S.A.
Telephone: 503/221-0836
Facsimile: 503/221-0837

Glimmer Train (ISSN #1055-7520) is published quarterly, $29 per year in the U.S., by Glimmer Train Press, Inc., Suite 1205, 812 SW Washington, Portland, OR 97205. Second-class postage paid at Portland, OR, and additional mailing offices. POSTMASTER: Send address changes to Glimmer Train Press, Inc., Suite 1205, 812 SW Washington, Portland, OR 97205.

ISSN # 1055-7520, ISBN # 1-880966-10-7, CPDA BIPAD # 79021

DISTRIBUTION: Bookstores can purchase *Glimmer Train Stories* through these distributors:
Bernhard DeBoer, Inc., 113 E. Centre St., Nutley, NJ 07110
Bookpeople, 7900 Edgewater Dr., Oakland, CA 94621
Ingram Periodicals, 1226 Heil Quaker Blvd., LaVergne, TN 37086
IPD, 674 Via de la Valle, #204, Solana Beach, CA 92075
Pacific Pipeline, 8030 S. 228th St., Kent, WA 98032
Ubiquity, 607 Degraw St., Brooklyn, NY 11217
SUBSCRIPTION SVCS: EBSCO, Faxon, READMORE

PRINTED IN U.S.A. ON RECYCLED, ACID-FREE PAPER.

Subscription rates: One year, $29 within the U.S. (Visa/MC/check).
Airmail to Canada, $39; outside North America, $49.
Payable by Visa/MC or check for U.S. dollars drawn on a U.S. bank.

Attention short-story writers: *We pay $300 for first publication and one-time anthology rights. Please include a self-addressed, sufficiently stamped envelope with your submission.* ***Manuscripts accepted in January, April, July, and October.*** *Send a SASE for guidelines, which will include information on our Short-Story Award for New Writers.*

Dedication

We honor our many readers
who have taken it upon themselves
to write letters requesting the release
of detained writers around the world.

This issue is dedicated to you.

Excerpts from letters written to PEN American Center:

I am writing to give you the good news that the five Greeks whose case you supported for more than a year have won their long fight against prosecution by the Greek government for treason! This is a great victory for free speech and freedom of the press in Greece. The five former defendants wish to extend their sincere thanks—they believe international support was vital to their victory.

Lance Selfa, on behalf of five Greek journalists

May I take this time to thank members of the American PEN Center for the campaign you mounted for my release. Words fail me to thank you sufficiently...for the magnitude of your members' fight for my effective life.

Malawian poet Jack Mapanje

Free, I am eager to salute your action which played an important role in bringing about my release. The efforts of the International PEN Club and your center's Freedom-to-Write Committee are instrumental not only in getting writers and intellectuals out of prisons but also in building a humanity based on justice and freedom ...

Moroccan essayist Abraham Serfaty

CONTENTS

Contents

Floyd Skloot

Forget the immaculate Tyrolean suit with its razor crease, the stiff, clunky shoes, the solid 1951 tricycle, even the sunny smile. This boy is holding on for dear life, as though he's about to be sucked straight up out of the picture.

Story Line Press will publish Floyd Skloot's second novel, *Summer Blue*, in the fall of 1994. His work has recently appeared in the *American Scholar, Shenandoah*, the *Virginia Quarterly Review*, the *Gettysburg Review*, the *Hudson Review, Midstream*, and the *Best American Essays of 1993*.

"The Fights" is from a recently completed novel, to be called *The Open Door*, about the Adler family—as was a previous story of Skloot's that *Glimmer Train* published in the spring of 1993.

FLOYD SKLOOT

The Fights

What a fall, what a winter. First, Roosevelt got reelected, trouncing Landon by eleven million votes. This was the best the Republicans could come up with, the governor of Kansas? Then, sit-down strikes spread like some kind of influenza out of Flint and soon half a million people were striking auto plants across the country. Plus, the Germans were still up to no good building the Siegfried Line, and you had a rebellion in Spain, and, all of a sudden, there was war between China and Japan. The world was a mess. It was forty-five below zero someplace in California, fifty below in Nevada! Even a subway World Series between the Giants and Yanks had done nothing to ease Myron Adler's nerves.

Which were shot anyway, after Sally O'Day.

He was not a particularly nervous man and he was not at all accustomed to following world news. But his time with Sally O'Day had changed Myron. She could fill an entire evening with talk about a guy named Gandhi teaching people to farm in India or about American troops pulling out of Haiti, which Myron never knew there were troops in. Starting when Sally slid into the car beside him, she'd carry on while they drove through the boroughs, sat in some nightclub for a few drinks, walked through a park or Coney Island, ate a dozen cherrystones. Sally couldn't believe Myron did not know where Ireland was exactly, or what her beef was with England. He'd felt proud of himself one night when, having accidentally listened to the news on the market's radio that afternoon, he mentioned that King George V had died. Sally flushed in an instant and began a string of curses against the king's soul that took Myron's breath away. It was like sticking your hand in a coop without paying attention; you could get nipped bad. Soon he began to read more than the sports section of the morning newspaper. He felt as though he were back in school again.

Myron met Sally O'Day at the fights in Rahway, January of 1934. God, was it really three years ago already? He wanted to marry her by Valentine's Day, and had even considered proposing in late September. But first, he would have to bring her home to meet his parents, and Myron hadn't quite figured out how to walk into the apartment in Brooklyn and announce to Emanuel and Sophia Adler that this blonde Irish girl was his intended. He could just see his mother, whose rhomboid face had yet to be cracked by any lines of habitual smiling, poised with utensils in midair, staring at his father, the would-be rabbi, the son of three generations of rabbis, who puts his knife and fork down with a careful clatter against the flowered Shabbos china, who looks up at them from under unruly brows—the only disorderly things in his life—closes his eyes, and with perhaps the hint of a smile says, "I don't believe so."

Myron would never forget that first night at the fights, when Sally's face floated up over her brother's shoulder like the moon. Si Sabbeth was still boxing then, though his loss to Carnera had ended any dreams they might have had of a championship bout. Of course, Myron was in his corner. It was snowing lightly; they'd already accepted the fact that there would be fewer than fifty people in the gym. Kid Sunday Si was scheduled for ten rounds against a guy from Queens called Matthew Monday. *Come to Rahway and see Sunday fight Monday on Tuesday the twenty-first!*

That evening at five, Si came down to Myron's market dressed in his usual fight-night leopard-skin coat that reached to his ankles. Despite his size, Si moved with the true grace of a great cat, especially when he wore the long coat. He'd walked through the doors without a sound and suddenly loomed over Florence Teitelbaum, who was waiting for her Tuesday pullets. She shrieked, leaping aside and losing her balance. She banged into the coops lining the market wall and was so upset that Myron gave her the birds for free.

Modulating his bass voice still lower, so that he seemed to be growling instead of speaking, Si apologized. "I'll pay you back out of the winnings tonight, Mashie."

Myron closed the market an hour early, throwing his bloody apron onto a pile in the back room by the plucking machines, whose odor he no longer smelled. "What the hell," he said, "you'll scare off all my customers anyway."

"You mean the weather will."

"Shaddup. Cold nights, people need their poultry even more."

As they drove out to Queens, the snow began. Myron flicked on the windshield wipers.

"It's a sign," Si murmured.

"Yeah, right. A sign we're gonna make about twelve bucks tonight."

"Wish I could have another shot at Carnera."

"He's fighting Loughran down in Miami in a couple months. Which it shoulda been you, a rematch. We could swing over to Havana after, have a nice little time, get some fresh cigars."

"What have I got, another couple years as a fighter, the most? I'm about old enough to be Matthew Monday's father, for Christ's sake. When boxing's over, I'm not even sure I could be in the poultry business. I'm through with blood."

"Look: A, you're gonna be in the wholesale end, not retail. So

B, you don't have to put your hands on a bird if you don't want to because C, you're gonna be an owner just like they agreed when you made that Carnera deal in the first place. So stop worrying. You fight this kid tonight and be ready to rock him back to sunny Ireland or wherever the hell they got him from."

"We'll see about this *owner* business. Those boys we dealt with, sometimes they have very short memories."

"I don't," Myron said. He took out a long Havana cigar and began to unwrap it with one hand. "There's a guy comes into the market every month or so; I mention it to him from time to time."

If there was a part of being in Si's corner that Myron hated, it was when they first entered the ring. He didn't mind sitting in the dressing room trying to keep Si's spirits up, taping his enormous hands, rubbing down his shoulders. He didn't mind tromping down the aisle to the ring and hearing the loudmouths blather. But once they were there, with his short arms Myron could barely hold the ropes apart far enough for Si to squeeze through, and then they had to stand together for the introductions. Like a clown act, with Myron maybe coming up to just past Si's solar plexus. He was much happier once the referee had told everybody the rules and sent them back to their corners. He got Si seated on the stool, spun out to straddle the post, and put his chin on Si's shoulder so they could both look across the ring at Matthew Monday and glower.

That's when he saw her. Sally's head of pale curls just rose into view, shrouded in smoke, as she stood to cheer her brother on. She was the most beautiful woman Myron had ever seen, despite a nose that looked as though it had been broken more often than her brother's and a thick scar that crossed her face—now crimson with excitement—running from the corner of her left eye to the center of her chin.

During the fight, Sally O'Day made Myron sloppy with his sponges and water. He conked Si's jaw with the spit bucket between rounds four and five. Drenched by a spray of sweat and spit and blood and water, forgetting to holler either encouragement or advice in Si's ear, smiling incongruously as the two fighters traded blows about six inches from his face, Myron was as dazed as Matthew ("Come on, Matty") Monday by the time Si put the kid down for good in the eighth.

"Great fight," he managed to say over the ringing of the bell.

"You were there?" Si answered. He leaned back against the ropes in his corner, waiting for the formal announcement of his victory, trying to get his breath back to normal.

"Come on, it was me that kept you together after the third round, which he almost had you with that uppercut."

While Myron untied the gloves, Si said, "In case you couldn't tell, that girl over there's no Jew. And your name's Myron, not Seamus."

"Ayyy, what makes you think I was looking at some girl? Everything I was looking at was between the ropes, which we had a fight going on."

Si snorted. "Mashie, I've known you since the third grade. Only thing is, she's not as bosomy as you like."

After the referee had held Si's hand up and the gym began to clear, Myron dallied in the corner, taking a long time to gather up their things. He watched Sally comforting her brother, helping him down from the ring, gazing after him as he made his way to the dressing room.

"Fought a nice fight, your brother."

She turned slowly, not seeing him at first, tracking the voice like a wary animal. "How big's your friend there, three-fifty, four hundred pounds? Fucking mismatch."

Sally liked Marx Brothers' movies and Charlie Chaplin. She enjoyed film biographies—Pasteur, Emile Zola. They went to see *Captains Courageous* and she swore Myron looked exactly like Spencer Tracy. In the first six months with her, Myron saw more films than he'd seen before in his whole life. She'd slouch beside him in the theater, legs over the seat in front of her, an arm around his shoulders, and munch on shelled peanuts smuggled in her purse. They'd pass a flask of whiskey back and forth. She was so slender, Myron couldn't account for her huge presence beside him. Her longshoreman's laugh filled the loge, as did her sobs, and she seemed to envelop him.

She loved to ride horses with him in Prospect Park. Sunday mornings, they'd meet at a diner in her neighborhood, Kinsella's, wolfing down their eggs-over-easy and fried potatoes so they could be at the stables early. Once, Myron reached across the table to dab at some yolk that was congealing in the scar near Sally's chin. She slapped his hand away hard, making him knock over her glass of grapefruit juice.

Before he could think—it had all happened so fast and the mood at their table had mutated so suddenly—Myron's hand had formed a fist and he was about to launch a right-cross at her. He froze. They stared at one another, hands still in the air, and didn't speak.

Finally, Sally looked down and said, "It was an accident, see. My father, you'll meet him someday, he was drunk. We went over the side of this road up near Tarrytown. There was a lot of glass. He wasn't scratched."

"Look, you know?" He gazed down at his hand as if it belonged to the table rather than to him. "I wouldn't really hit you. I mean, I don't know."

"It's all right." In a moment, she looked back up at him. "At least you didn't follow through."

Sally wanted to ride a different horse each week. Myron, who always rode the same thick palomino named Zev, after the '23 Derby winner, thought Sally lacked discipline on a horse. But he liked to watch her gallop and to see the smile it brought to her face, the only time smiling actually transversed her scar to include the entire face.

One spring morning while they were cantering, she shot away from him. She was on a flashy bay named Burnt Sienna, who was known around the stables as headstrong. Myron, still sluggish from breakfast, was slow to react and Zev was confused beneath him. It was five or six seconds before they took off after her. He could see that Sally was almost out of control, maybe because of the wind, maybe because she was distracted by how far ahead she'd gotten. Although it was invisible from where she was, he knew she was nearing where the path would plunge downhill and suddenly cross a street heavy with churchgoing traffic. This was no place to be galloping. There were signs, but she wasn't likely to read them and it was useless to call to her. He began to catch up. Then Myron saw that the wind was toying with her hat. She straightened in her saddle and Burnt Sienna slowed slightly. Myron urged Zev on and was close enough behind her that, when the hat blew off, he leaned down and snatched it out of the air.

"My hero," Sally said, laughing as they came to a stop.

Myron put her hat on his head, where it just managed to cover his bald spot like a yarmulke. Their horses were edgy, wanting to run again. Sally reached down to stroke Burnt Sienna's neck. Myron was sure she'd be bucked off in an instant, but he'd learned by now not to try controlling her horse. He kept his hands to himself.

"I like you better without the hat," he said.

"Myron Adler, what a bold thing to say to a lass. And on a Sunday, no less."

They began to walk along the trail again, headed down toward the street. "I think you'd better stay with me," Myron said.

"And why should I do that?"

"I know these paths. And besides, you're a little wild."

They reached the street, holding up traffic while they clopped across. Then she turned to fix him with a smile. "Exactly, my brilliant. And wild is why you'll keep chasing me."

She took off again. Myron laughed out loud. Before he went after her, he tucked Sally's hat into his belt.

A little over a year later, Si had a bout scheduled for April twelfth, a true Friday-night fight, the best card he'd been on since Carnera. They'd have to drive to Philly and stay overnight, but it would be worth doing. Si was actually smiling again, at least once in a while, and talking about putting enough money aside to buy a little place near Sheepshead Bay.

Training was the worst time for Myron because he had to squeeze roadwork in before he opened the market at five-thirty in the morning. Now that he was seeing Sally in the evenings, Myron was always exhausted when he met Si at four-thirty in the park.

Si's voice rumbled out of the depths of his toweled, hooded head. "You don't look so good."

"And you look like a peccadillo in that getup, so don't give me any crap."

Myron handed Si two socks filled with weights. They began to jog along the same bridle paths Myron had ridden with Sally. Every quarter mile or so, Si would throw a few punches at the air, turn to dance a few steps backward, then spin forward again, still jabbing away. Myron would run loops around him during those interludes, chanting, "Keep it up. Keep it up."

"So what's new with you and Our Lady of the Mondays?" Si said.

"Let's talk strategy, okay?"

"You're not supposed to have strategies in love."

"I'm talking about your fight, Simon. You know, the reason we're out here in the middle of the night, which I should be asleep right now."

Si was moving backward again, with Myron circling him and feinting punches of his own. "I mean it, Mashie. What's going on with you two? It's been, what, sixteen months? I haven't met her yet."

"*Keep it up. Keep it up.* Jesus, nothing's going on. We just keep to ourselves. I haven't met none of her friends and none of her family, myself."

"That's not technically true. If I recall, there was her brother, young 'Look Out Matty,' around that first night. Hey, maybe that's it. He probably doesn't like the friends you keep. She neither. Is that why I haven't had the honor?"

"What're you talking about? Come on, let's do the miles. I gotta get to the market."

Si reached out to grab Myron's arm and they stopped jogging. "What is going on! Why don't I meet her? Why don't your parents? Why don't you meet her people? And why the hell did you just call me Simon? I've known you since we were nine and that's the first time you ever called me Simon. What did you do, knock her up?"

"Shaddup." Myron turned away, hunched his shoulders, jogged in place. "It's just, well, I... Jesus, *Si*, we got some roadwork to do."

The night before the fight, April the eleventh, Myron closed the market early again. He scrubbed up in the back room but there wasn't any soap left and he couldn't get all the dried blood out from under his fingernails. He knew he smelled like gizzards. Good thing he wasn't going to see Sally tonight. And tomorrow he didn't want to think about. Which there was no choice, he had to leave it up to Gabriel Kozey to run the place tomorrow while they were in Philly, to open it on time, to keep it open all day. And it was Friday, no less! *Shabbos*, when all his best customers would come in for their Sabbath chickens.

He walked up the street without seeing anything, all his concentration focused inward on the horror of what would probably happen tomorrow in the market. The floor would be filthy. Gabe would forget to put down fresh sawdust during the day and there would be clots of blood everywhere. He'd be rude to women who weren't pretty enough, and the birds would not be properly drained. So when Myron, sunk in a morbid despair, reached the car, he was astonished to find Sally leaning against the driver's door.

"What's this?" he said.

"This is a valise."

"That's not what I mean. What're you doing here?"

Sally's eyes narrowed. "Don't be ridiculous, all right? Just open the door, I don't want to stand here like this."

"Look, we're going to Philly, you know that. Si's got a fight, which we sleep in some cheap joint afterward and then come home."

"I know all that. Jeez, I thought you'd be happy I was coming with you."

"It's no place for a girl."

She put her elbows on the hood of the car and stared at him. Myron held her stare.

"I grew up around fights, Myron. Maybe you remember where we first met? And I'm not only coming to Philly, I'm coming to that holy chicken market of yours when we get back. I want to see you in the real world."

Myron was shaking his head as he unwrapped a cigar and bit off the end. He wouldn't look at her.

"Besides," he said.

"Besides, nothing. It's time I got to know Si as somebody other than a gorilla who tore my Matty apart."

He walked around the car, unlocked the passenger door, and waited for Sally to get in. Then he squatted down and leaned in next to her. "Si and me, we do a certain way before he fights. Which we haven't done it any different for maybe ten years."

"Like what?"

"Okay, just tell me this. Where you gonna sleep?"

"Why, Si usually sleeps in the bed with you?"

When they stopped in front of Si's apartment, he was just locking the door. His enormous, leopard-skinned back filled the doorway. He turned, grinning, with two cigars stuck in his

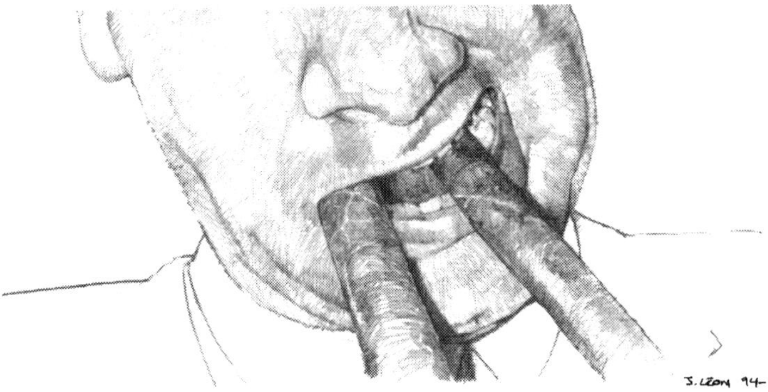

mouth and pointing skyward. When he saw Sally next to Myron in the car, both cigars dove toward the ground.

He tried to climb into the back seat and couldn't make it, so he stepped out, turned around and tried to back in. That didn't work either. "I'm terribly sorry, but either you have to grease me or Miss O'Day sits in the back."

For the first fifty or sixty miles, they couldn't get a conversation to last for more than a minute at a time unless it was about directions and route numbers. Finally, Si squirmed halfway around in his seat, trying to look at Sally with both eyes, but could only manage to turn far enough to see her with one.

"Miss O'Day, I have to ask you something. I tried asking Mashie over here, but that's like talking to a radish when something like this comes up. Okay?"

"On one condition, Mr. Sabbeth. From here on, you call me Sally and I call you Si. Unless you'd prefer Kid."

Si smiled. "Tell me, Sally, where do your parents think you are every night you go out with Mashie?"

"Jesus Christ," Myron said. He looked quickly at Si, then back out at the road ahead. "I mean, Jesus Christ."

"No, that's a fair question, Myron," Sally said. "They think I'm at political rallies, Si, sometimes at discussion groups, that sort of thing. Sinn Féin."

"You're kidding me," Myron said. "They don't know about me at all?"

"I don't believe this," Sally said. "And where does your family think you are?"

Suddenly, Myron had to change lanes, which took an extraordinary amount of concentration. He took a quick peek at Si, who was still torqued around in his seat and looked as though he might never be able to straighten out again.

"I mean it, Myron," Sally said. "Where?"

"All right, all right. I get the point."

"Where!"

"They think I'm with Si a lot, which we're looking for a place to open a market together. Or I'm playing poker a couple times a week. Work on the books."

"Boy," Sally said. "You, too."

"Take a left here," Si said. The rest of the way, they talked about the Baer-Braddock fight, which was coming up in a couple months. They talked about the sorry Brooklyn Dodgers, who looked about as bad as last year except, thank God, for Van Lingle Mungo and Watty Clark. They listened to Sally talk about *Mutiny on the Bounty* and some discussion program she liked to listen to on the radio. They got a good twenty minutes out of the Delaware River.

From the moment they entered the arena, nothing went right. The dressing room didn't have anything big enough for Si to lie down on except the floor, there wasn't enough tape, and the fight before Si's ended with a first-round knockout so they had to hurry to get ready.

Myron knew Si was in trouble as soon as the opening bell rang. He wasn't moving right, as though he still had the weighted socks around his shoulders, and he was a half second slow. The guy was nailing him with jabs. What was it, had they overtrained? Si was actually five pounds light; they thought he could use the extra sharpness. Maybe they'd done too much roadwork. Si missed a roundhouse right and almost flipped out of the ring.

Between the fourth and fifth rounds, Myron finally said, "What's wrong, Si? Just make him come to you and nail him with a left hook. He's wide open."

"There's nothing there, Mashie. Maybe I should sit on him."

Myron had never seen Si get knocked down before. Except for the Carnera fight, and all that knocked him down then was a promise. When Si hit the canvas on his back, arms flopping over his head, tears rushed into Myron's eyes, which astonished him even more than the sight of his friend prone and being counted out.

They ate dinner in a small cafe near the hotel—soup all around, since Si didn't feel like chewing and Myron and Sally weren't hungry. They sopped up the last bits with soft white bread, looking into their bowls, not speaking much.

Myron took care of room arrangements while Sally held Si by the elbow on the front stairs. Si stayed in a room down the hall from them. He bid them good night and walked slowly away, a hand up to wave, without really looking back.

Inside the room, Myron went directly over to the window and looked down at the street. Sally sat on the bed. He was still except for the clenching and unclenching of his hands.

"He'll be fine, Myron. Time alone's good for him tonight."

"Maybe. But did you see him there? I mean," he turned back to her, "Si on the floor, you know?"

"I know. Come here."

As he began to sit beside her, Sally turned toward Myron and wrapped her arms around him, throwing his back onto the bed while his legs dangled over the edge. She straddled him. She took off his glasses and leaned over his head to put them on the bedside table, her breasts moving across his face.

Myron reached up for her. Sally gripped his wrists, lowered his hands to the bed and spread them wide.

"Be still," she whispered.

"I..."

"Be still, Myron."

He woke up at about four and Sally was staring at him, her breast against his, her fingers tangled in his chest hair. They were still on top of the blanket, still naked.

"What?" he asked.

Sally closed her eyes. Gently, she shook her head and put it down against his shoulder.

"This was different," Myron said. "This was very different."

"Yes."

One Sunday in early May of 1936, Myron drove Sally to the south shore of Long Island for an afternoon at the beach. He had been to this small resort town of Long Beach before and jogged along its boardwalk a few times with Si when they wanted someplace different for Sunday roadwork. Afterward, they'd eat a couple dozen clams and drink beers on the bay side of town.

Today, though, was not about training or eating clams. In the evening, they would go to Myron's home and finally have dinner with his family. Emanuel and Sophia didn't seem surprised when Myron said he wanted to bring a girl home to meet them. Apparently, Myron's sisters had long suspected he was seeing someone; it had been a topic of their dinnertime conversation for quite a while.

He took Sally's hand and led them east on the boardwalk. It was windy and cool for May. Sally's face was bright red before they'd walked two blocks.

"You wanna go into the Jackson there and have some coffee?" Myron asked. "Maybe this wasn't such a bright idea I had."

"I'm fine. Only let's get down onto the sand."

He led her down the ramp at the next corner and turned back to pass underneath the boardwalk. The sand there was dark gray and cold when they took off their shoes and socks. Once out from under the planks, though, the sand seemed much warmer than the air. They headed east again, moving slowly through the softness.

"The water looks unbearable," Sally said.

"Not if you don't go into it."

"Myron, you have to use your imagination."

"I left it in the glove compartment. Look, Sally, I got a question for you."

She pulled him closer and put her arm around his waist. "And I have the answer: chopped liver. It's probably the only thing I refuse to eat and it's exactly what I think they're going to serve."

He stopped. "I been thinking about this for a long time, all right? I mean, would you wanna marry me?"

Myron could actually see the redness fade from her skin, as though he'd thrown bleach in her face instead of asked her to marry him. But wait, it wasn't that. What was happening was all the red from her face was seeping into her eyes.

"Mother of God, Myron."

"Hey, I don't speak Irish, remember? Does that mean yes or no?"

"Shouldn't we wait to see what your parents think? Or mine?"

"It won't matter."

Sally took a step to the side, still holding his hand. She looked away, watching a wave die out in foam. "Yes."

"You will?"

"No. I mean, yes, I will. But I was saying yes, it will matter. To me, anyway."

For the rest of the afternoon in Long Beach, they were shy together. It wasn't how Myron thought it would be, after you asked a girl to marry you. They drove back into Brooklyn early, got dressed early, and arrived at the Adlers' apartment forty minutes ahead of schedule. From the hallway, they could smell the roasting chickens. No liver, he was sure of it.

As though they knew he'd be early, Emanuel and Sophia were fully dressed and standing together in the foyer when Myron opened the door and led Sally in. Emanuel had on his best cardigan, a deep piney green one, and Sophia wore the ruffly blue dress with millions of buttons that Myron always loved. He was deeply touched.

After the introductions, they went into the living room where Myron's sisters were waiting for them—Hannah, Charlotte, and even Bella, who was married and lived in Trenton. Of course, his brothers Herb and Joseph were not there, that would have been too much. A wedding, yes, or a funeral, but this was just to meet a girl they didn't know he'd been seeing for over two years. Of course, Myron hadn't brought home many girls at all.

"So tell me, dear," Sophia said when they had all been introduced and served their crackers, "where did you two meet?"

"In New Jersey, Mrs. Adler. I was at a function there with my brother."

Oh, very good, Myron thought. There's plenty of time to talk boxing.

The evening went splendidly. Bella knew about the issues of Irish unification and British colonialism. Charlotte had read *Gone with the Wind.* Hannah was the same size as Sally and also loved to sew. Myron stole glances at his parents, who were smiling as though he'd brought home someone named Rose Goldberg.

Emanuel was waiting for him when Myron returned after driving Sally home. It was two a.m.

"Pop, you waited up."

Emanuel nodded. "Your mother and I wanted you to know how pleased we are that you brought Miss O'Day home to meet us. And she's a lovely young lady. I can see why you're attracted to her."

"It's more than that, you know. We've been seeing a lot of each other."

"I thought as much."

Myron walked past his father into the dining room and sat at his usual dinnertime place. "It's— I'm— We're pretty serious." He looked down the table as though wondering where the succotash had gone. "I want to marry her, Pop."

"You do." Emanuel sat at the table's head and folded his hands where his plate should be. "I can certainly understand why, too, seeing her and listening to her. Very sharp, she is. But you know it would be impossible."

Myron looked at him. "It's 1936, Pop. Brooklyn, not Cracow."

"This I know. But in our family, Myron, you cannot do what you're thinking of doing." He spread his hands on the table.

"Cannot."

"I'm twenty-eight years old. I own a business."

"In a building that I own, Myron."

Emanuel was watching the kitchen door as though expecting Sophia to emerge with a platter of flanken. Myron was looking across the table, to where his sister Charlotte used to sit and gorge herself with food while talking about losing weight.

"What are you saying, Pop?"

"Only what you heard, Myron. Nothing more or less."

What a spring, what a summer. Travel was on everyone's mind, getting away, moving on, going fast as possible. Down in Lakehurst, New Jersey, not an hour away from Myron's market, the zeppelin *Hindenburg* burst into flames at its tower mooring. People in midtown Manhattan who wanted to see where thirty-five zeppelin passengers and crew had died could take the new Lincoln Tunnel under the Hudson River and surface in Weehawken five minutes later. When Myron first drove through the tunnel to look at a new supplier of fowl, he held his breath almost the whole way. Over on the West Coast, the Golden Gate Bridge opened and, somewhere in the South Pacific, Amelia Earhart disappeared in her little plane. Meanwhile, Howard Hughes was flying around the world in less than four days. But Myron knew there was no place to go.

When he told Sally they couldn't see each other again, it was as though she already knew what he was going to say. She kissed him passionately and ran her fingers along his cheek about where her own scar would be if it were on his face.

"It matters," she said. "I always knew it matters."

MARGARET ATWOOD

Canadian novelist, poet, short-story writer

Interview

by Linda Davies

The author of sixteen volumes of poetry, ten novels (including **The Handmaid's Tale** *and her just-released* **The Robber Bride***), and four short-story collections, Margaret Atwood has won numerous awards and is certainly one of North America's favorite writers. She lives in Toronto with her writer husband, Graeme Gibson, and their daughter, Jess.*

Margaret Atwood

DAVIES: *What do you remember about being seven years old?*

ATWOOD: I can actually remember quite a bit about it. My life until I was twelve really came in two parts: summer, fall, and spring, when we were living in the north woods; and winter, when we were living in the city. During the city part, I was living on the outskirts of Toronto in postwar housing. It would have been just after the end of the Second World War.

I can remember that I could not have pets because we had this

Glimmer Train Stories, Issue 11, Summer 1994

double life. So, instead, I had a caterpillar. It must have been the fall.

Really?

Yeah. I had a caterpillar in a jar. That was my pet.

What was that like?

Well, you know. I later had a praying mantis as a pet. They're quite intelligent. You can teach them how to drink sugar water out of a spoon. They don't live very long; none of those things do.

And we used to go out and hunt for mice. There were a lot of mice around there because it was a place that was just being developed with a lot of open fields and, of course, where there are open fields there are mice.

I had the mumps at that time. I can remember that very clearly. The next-door neighbor gave me a balloon. Now, you must understand that there had been no balloons during the war because rubber was rationed, so this was a very old balloon. It was from before the war and it was the only balloon I had ever seen. I had heard of balloons in stories; I knew there were such things, but I'd never actually seen one. So we blew this balloon up and it existed for about one second and then, because it was so old, it burst.

Were you heartbroken?

Yes, but nevertheless, I had had that balloon for one instant. Now, do you want any other heartrending stories?

Do you have something else in mind?

Well, nothing like that, but I had an older brother and we mostly were engaged in various devious activities at that time, as I recall.

You enjoyed each other?

Oh yes, quite a lot. So, that's about what I was doing. In the summers we were on Lake Superior by then, and that was a great deal of fun except that you had to be very careful not to go out too far because you might get swept away by the current. It was at this point where Lake Superior gets more narrow, so the current was picking up then.

So you had a wonderful, outdoor childhood experience?

During the summers, yes.

In the winters, I guess it's too cold to think about being outside.

Well, not if you're dressed properly. My daughter, Jess, took winter holiday to go on an Outward Bound winter-wilderness course for ten days north of Thunder Bay, which is at the end of Lake Superior. It was fifty-two below, and she loved it! Dogsled running and cross-country skiing with her tuna sandwiches under her arm to warm them up enough so that she could eat them. Life in the wilderness.

How is your life different now than you anticipated it would be when you were twenty-two and publishing your first collection of poems?

I self-published my first book, but I wasn't twenty-two. I was twenty-one. People always get my age wrong because my birthday's in November, so they think I'm a year older than I am.

Oh, right. You probably had expectations about what your life would be like. How is it different?

In Canada at that time, it was not really possible for anyone to make a living writing. I would say the possibility now is about the same as it is in the States, namely ten percent, but it is a possibility. At that time, which was about 1961, there were very few Canadian publishers and the few who did exist were reluctant to publish novels by Canadian authors because they thought it was too much of a risk. I think in 1960 there were five books published the entire year in English-language Canada by Canadian authors and about twenty books of poetry, which would include pamphlets and little things like that. So my expectations were quite low. I certainly thought that I would have to go to a more cosmopolitan place where there was more of an audience. It was usual for Canadians of my generation to go to London, because they could get into it more easily than they could get into the States, believe it or not. Then things calmed down and it became equally difficult either way. I ended up, in fact, going to Harvard instead of to England. I thought I might be a literary writer and have an audience of maybe a thousand people. That's about as far as it went. So I had more of a John Keats idea of myself—starving in the garrets, writing masterpieces, dying of TB—you know, those romantic kinds of things.

Is this less romantic but much more satisfying?

Well, of course the older you get the more you appreciate having, for instance, your own bathroom. I lived in rooming houses for a while, and I'm not sure I could do that now with the alacrity with which I did it then. I think I've done the rooming-house days of my life.

So, things have certainly turned out very much differently than from what I expected at the time.

More favorably?

Much more favorably. I thought that I would always have to have a day job and write in the evening. I did that for a long time, and I'm just as glad not to have to do it, particularly with a family. If you have a day job, a family, and you try to write, that's really about one more thing than you can manage.

Do you think that you're much more productive without that stress?

Oh, no doubt about it. I taught university for years. You can write poetry under those circumstances, but it's very difficult to write long prose fiction.

Your daughter is seventeen now?

Yes, she is.

When you look at her, in what ways do you see your mother?

My mother? Now, that's interesting. First of all, my daughter is quite athletic, and so was my mother. My mother was a very keen horseback rider and when they moved out to the north woods, where there was no possibility of horseback riding, she took up other pursuits. She was a very good canoeist, for instance. She was always a person who very much liked the outdoors. That's true of me, too. I used to teach woodcraft at summer camp and take canoe trips and stuff like that. Because we grew up there, we all knew how to do things like light a fire with one match in a rainstorm. My daughter started horseback riding when she was seven. She started to ride in England when we were living there and she continued it up until this year. She really liked it a lot, so that was something she did that was like my mother.

Was that a pleasure to see, that continuity?

I think it was very pleasurable for my mother. She used to go watch her ride and jump and do those things.

And, in yourself, where do you see your father?

Well, my father was very curious about all kinds of things, and that's certainly a quality I share with him. He was very interested in history, and so am I. He was a person who questioned things a lot, so this was the atmosphere of the household. There was quite a lot of discussion that went on all the time and there were always a lot of books around, a lot of history books. I would say that that side of me comes from him rather than from my mother.

And it's obviously a source of great pleasure to you.

It's a source of pleasure to me and was a source of pleasure to him.

In an earlier interview you'd said that each person has a story, a personal narrative that is constantly replayed and revised. Would you be willing to name a couple of significant aspects of your own personal narrative at this time?

Well, the thing about novelists is that they more or less duck the issue of their personal narratives while constructing narratives for other people. In a way, the personal narrative of the writer is not really a personal narrative; it is connected with all of the narratives of these other people. In other words: What was I doing in 1992? Was I living my personal narrative or was I living the personal narrative of the three characters I was involved in? You can't really separate them. When I think about what I was doing at the time, well, some of the time I was having lunch and going for walks, but at the same time, all of the time, I was engaged with these other people. The writer lives multiple narratives and that's what makes the writer different from the person who is not a writer, who is usually just working on one story—namely, their own.

You also mentioned how important you feel it is to be financially independent.

Yes.

Did you learn that from a particular person?

I learned that from my family. They had been through the Depression, number one. Number two, my parents' attitude—they were both from Nova Scotia—is of quite an independent-minded culture: 'You have the brains—you should use them.' Their attitude was not: 'You're a girl—you can't do it.' I never had any of that. Instead, I had the idea that they weren't rich and if I was going to do what I wanted to do, I would have to earn the money to do it. I had my first job when I was eight, wheeling the neighbors' baby around. That's part of my personal narrative that I've been able to use. I put it in *Cat's Eye.*

I had another job when I was twelve, working at the community center, and I went on to develop, with one of my friends, a puppet business that we ran in high school. We actually got quite good. We had an agent at one point who booked us into these Christmas shows the companies did for their employees and families. We put on the classics, "The Three Little Pigs," "Little Red Riding Hood," and "Hansel and Gretel." We made all the puppets ourselves and we made the stage and we did the lighting and we made the costumes.

You had a business!

We had a business, yeah. We were earning at one point what was then the astronomical sum of twenty-five bucks a show. This was big. I had my little bank account. Then I had summer jobs. And so it went on.

I had a silk-screen business in college. I did silk-screen posters for events such as the Gilbert and Sullivan productions, *The Plays*, some formal dances. You know how serigraphy works?

No.

Well, you have a piece of silk that is stretched on a frame and you block out the parts of it that you don't want the paint to go through—there are various methods of doing that—then you put the color that you want on the top and you squeegee over things. That makes that color. You let that dry and then, to make the next color, you have to line it all up and push it through again. Now, with color Xerox, it's a thing of the past. So, I had that business and it was certainly preferable to selling in Woolworth's. I was always a somewhat enterprising child.

Did either of your parents have a business as such?

No. My father was a scientist. My mother was my mother. She had been a dietitian at one point.

So, this entrepreneurial streak of yours, where did it come from?

Well, my father had been an enterprising person. He had come from a backwoods farm in Nova Scotia, and how he became a scientist is a whole other story. He more or less worked his way from stepping stone to stepping stone and ended up with a degree in entomology, teaching at the University of Toronto. It was during the Depression as well, so, as you can imagine, he really had to hustle.

We have the women's movement. We have the men's movement. Will we resolve ourselves eventually?

Well, the way the United States seems to be organized at the moment in all areas of culture and society, it seems to be run along adversarial lines. In other words, there's a lot of: 'I will express my right by either attacking you or suing you and that is how I will establish what is right for me to have, and the reason I have to do that is that you are not going to concede it otherwise—the only thing I can get for myself is what I can get through adversarial methods.' This is really unfortunate, although it makes a lot of work for lawyers. I think it might be very good for everybody to go and get the Harvard negotiating team book called *Getting to Yes without Backing Down*, which points out that there cannot be a negotiation unless there's some good to be had for both sides. Otherwise, unless you're willing for your opponent, or the person you conceive to be your opponent, to get something good, too, there will not be a negotiation.

A very obvious statement, now that you have made it.

They make many obvious statements in their book that people have not thought very much about. So that is what I think people should maybe work on now—namely, the concept of mutual good rather than the concept of absolute right.

Perhaps that answers another question I intended to ask you. When we hear about violence, if it's a little removed it's somewhat less shocking. In the Portland School District on Monday, one twelve-year-old boy stabbed another twelve-year-old boy at school, nearly to death. I wondered if your perspective as a Canadian—looking at the American violence that we have—if you have some ...

We've got violence, too.

To the same degree, do you think?

Well, no, because we have stricter gun-control laws. There is a kind of rule of thumb which was set forth by Konrad Lorenz when he was talking about aggression. If you wish to kill somebody, the more bodily contact that's involved, the harder it is for you to do that. In other words, it's much harder to strangle somebody than it is to shoot them. So when people throw temper tantrums, if they don't have weapons, fewer deaths result. It's more just sort of bonking people on the nose. Violence is happening, but the results are not so fatal. Once you have weapons such as guns and knives, it makes it much easier to do harm at a distance. Easiest of all is to press a button and, thousands of miles away, something explodes. It's psychologically easier to do that, and that's why it's more dangerous and why much stricter controls have to be exercised. So, I would say the United States is going to have to come to grips with the proliferation of its domestic arsenal.

With all these weapons lying around, some kids are going to get hold of them and some kids are going to use them because they see it on TV all the time.

And, on TV, the harm is not fully seen.

You don't see the consequences. When you kill somebody you're not just killing them, you're affecting their entire family and everybody who knows them.

We are in the final years of this millennium. Do you have any idea what this decade might look like fifty years from now?

It will probably look like the beginning of the twenty-first century. I would say that the twenty-first century began in 1989, when walls came down. We had the twentieth century from about 1914 until 1989. That's when world order shifted in an unforeseeable way. We don't know what the outcome is going to be, but it is not going to be like the past fifty years.

I've seen you described as unflappable, and you do seem very comfortable. Does that description fit you?

Well, unflappable is not true of anyone. Anyone can be flapped. It depends on the occasion. Me, I don't like thunderstorms because they were the big menace when I was growing up—thunderstorms, forest fires, were very scary stuff. We have violent thunderstorms in the north of Canada. They hit things and cause fires, and I really don't like them very much. Urban people, who have grown up in cities, would probably find that quite funny.

How have you acquired your sense of ease?

Well, I'm quite old, you know. I've been doing this for quite a long time and when I'm dealing with people who have to make a speech and they're not used to it and they're very nervous, what I say to them is: 'Whatever you do up there, even if you trip over the microphone wire, lose your glasses, spill your water, they'll all think it's part of the act. Anyway, they're there to hear you and, therefore, they want you to be good and they want to like you, so why worry?'

So, you simply recognize that. At twenty-one, did you recognize that?

Well, I began reading my poetry in a coffeehouse, which you may see described in a story of mine called "Lightness and Darkness." It's pretty much the coffeehouse as it was. It was called the Bohemian Embassy. It was very dark and we had the Chianti bottles with the candles in them and the checked tablecloths and the folk singing interlude. The washrooms opened onto the main room where you read. They also had an espresso machine, one of the first espresso machines ever seen by anybody in this group, and it was highly regarded. Just as you would reach your most moving line, somebody would be sure to either turn on the espresso machine or flush the toilet and open the door. So, after that, nothing has ever been quite as bad.

The worst thing that can happen to you when you're doing a public performance is that the microphone system can fail.

I was doing a reading in Miami one time, and the podium shrank. It was broken. It was one of those things that moves up and down, and, as I was reading, it just got smaller and smaller. I wondered, *Am I finally growing?* I then had to yank it up and start again, and it got smaller again. Finally, in the middle of the reading, they walked out with a different podium.

How distracting!

I know, but these things just happen—a lot—and you just have to handle them as they come along. I think white-water canoeing is really good practice for things like that.

Excerpts from
United States Department of Agriculture
Farmers' Bulletin #1099
Issued June 1920, Reprinted June 1922

HOME LAUNDERING.

BOILING.

Boiling helps in cleaning soiled clothes, but they should be well washed first. Most clothes need only about five minutes of actual boiling; too long tends to yellow the cloth. Kerosene, turpentine, or shaved paraffin may be added if the clothes are very dirty or yellowed. If kerosene is used, the clothes should be thoroughly rinsed in order to remove the odor. This is equally the case with turpentine, the odor of which is even more objectionable to many persons, so much so that it is sometimes believed to cause illness; it is also sometimes considered injurious to the hands.

IRONS.

If old-fashioned flatirons are used, at least three should be provided. This allows a change of iron often enough to rest the hand and keep the irons hot.

Electric, gas, gasoline, and alcohol irons save the worker from standing near a fire and from walking back and forth to change irons.

In buying an electric iron, choose one made by a recognized electrical supply company. The electric wires that lead from the iron should be watched; if any break appears in the covering, it can easily be mended with adhesive tape while the current is off. These breaks should not remain uncared for, because of the danger of shock and fire.

Gas, gasoline, and alcohol irons burn fuel within the iron. Care must be used with the last two because if the container leaks, fire will result.

A mangle is of great help; if one can not afford both that and a washing machine, one should get the latter first, because there are more clothes to wash than flat pieces to iron. Only sheets, pillowcases, table linen, and underwear without buttons or ruffles should be put through a mangle.

FIG. 7.—Cold mangle.

Tiziana di Marina Lohnes

Left to right: my brother Donnie, my father Rick, me, my mother Maria, and my sister Laura, in a pizza parlor in Italy, sometime in late 1977. I've always had a need to be completely enclosed by my family; even now, I find that I have little sense of "self" which is separate from them.

Tiziana (pronounced Tee-tsee-ah-nah) Lohnes was born on February 25, 1972, in Naples, Italy, where she was raised by her mother and maternal relatives until the age of seven, when she and her nuclear family moved to the United States. "La Donna E Mobile" is the title piece from an unpublished collection of short stories.

Lohnes often finds creative inspiration in howling at the full moon with a few close friends at her side.

Tiziana di Marina

TIZIANA DI MARINA

La Donna E Mobile

Nonna responds that the events of her life amount to a pile of pins that she has kept in a dresser for the last four decades. "Pins." Nonna repeats it in case I have missed her peculiar retort. "Pins."

Nonna's life is said to have started at the moment that Nonno found her on the street all alone with a red rose pinned into the end of her hair. Nonno strolled past Nonna and he did not even have a look at her face before he fell in love with her. Her hair was a deep red then and it has become a less severe red now because of the streaks of white that started to blend in with it five summers before this summer. But it is clear that Nonna once had beautiful masses of hair that fell all around her shoulders, that it was this blanket of hair that enticed Nonno the first time that he found her on the streets of Naples alone and he asked her to be his wife.

These are some of the facts that I know about Nonna and these are the small colorful pebbles that I scoop up and hide in the pockets of these peasant skirts that I wear in the summer heat. Nonna is Mamma's Mamma. Her life is said to have started at the moment that Nonno saw her and claimed her from behind on the street. Nonno used to walk in Naples in the summer breeze and Nonna used to walk in Naples in the summer breeze, too, but neither one had seen the other until this time that he noticed the red rose in the red hair. This time both of them walked in

Glimmer Train Stories, Issue 11, Summer 1994

the summer breeze, Nonna in front and Nonno behind her the entire time. It was her hair that he had fallen in love with and as the breeze tried to lift it off her shoulders Nonno noted the resistance of the thick red braid to the feeble attempts of this little piece of air. The braid reached as far down as the smallest curve in her back and never moved once even as she walked across those busiest streets in which Nonno found her.

Nonno followed her and followed her and he said to himself that he would be married to that redhead before the end of the month. Nonno chased Nonna first to the baker. He did not dare follow her inside. But Nonna never came out from the door in which she had entered and Nonno realized in a panic that Nonna must have left out the back door and that he'd never find her in the street. Nonno rushed on the path to the market (the direction that this road led) and detected the red braid and the red rose at the fruit stands. Nonno had come so near behind Nonna that he could have taken a bite out of the loaf of bread that she held in one of her hands and rested on her left shoulder.

Nonna asked the old woman behind the stand about the freshness of her pomegranates. The fruit looked ripe and red to Nonna. Nonna could even taste its sweetness in her mouth as she felt it and held it up to her nose and smelled it. Nonna desired one, but she had absorbed the latest medicinal folk tale that said that women who ate the fruit birthed children with red marks (in the form of the fruit) on their faces.

Nonna had never even had a suitor before (but for Nonno, of course, and she did not even know about him as she stood in front of the fruit stand), but she asked the old woman about the children and the birthmarks. Nonna had turned nineteen that week and she carried herself about town with a red rose in her thick red French braid after all and would soon have suitors. The old version of the folk tale that Nonna had been raised on had been that it was women with babies in their stomachs who should not eat the flesh of that thick red fruit because its enormous seeds would either scratch and mar the faces of the children in the womb or the children in the womb would choke on the seed and die. But the red fruit had become more scarce than ever that summer and the most recent fable claimed that no woman who planned to have children in the future should even touch them. It was too bad for Nonna and for others because it had been these unmarried and married ladies who wanted to have children who craved the fruit the most.

Nonna had been at the market talking to the old woman behind the fruit stand about pomegranates when the old woman had opened her wrinkled mouth to respond but had instead choked on a pin that she had in her mouth between her old teeth. The old woman started to turn blue and Nonna screamed for assistance and this was the moment that Nonno vaulted over the fruit stand to the old woman and started to pound on her back in order to force her to take a breath. Nonna remained at the fruit stand until she was certain that the old woman was well and then she turned to finish her errands.

Nonno, in the excitement of it all, had still not seen Nonna's face. He reassured himself nonetheless that Nonna would be his wife as he saw her thick braid turn around and head for the fish markets in the near distance. Nonna on the other hand had seen his face (and it was not a bad face as far as faces went) but because he had still not seen her face (also not too bad as far as faces went) Nonna continued to reel him in like a fish after her on those streets. It was the red French braid that he could see, after all, as massive as a mulatto's hair and as lush as shoe polish, and it reached to the bottom of her back. I can see that Nonna's life had been at a standstill until the moment that Nonno claimed her, and her red hair, and the rose pinned into the red hair, as all his.

Nonno followed Nonna to the fish markets until he almost fell at her heels but Nonno could not see that it was he who looked like a fish at that moment, like a fish that Nonna could choose for dinner. He seemed like an uncertain fish because he could not decide if he wanted to see the face of the fisherwoman who had lured him to shore or not.

Before Nonna chose a fish at the fish market the two of them saw a thin child lift salted anchovies from a small barrel and run off before he was found out. Both of them remembered in unison the proverb that their mothers had told them in childhood: there is never a "small theft"; that the child who steals a fish at the market becomes the child who steals coins and then bills from his mother's purse; that this child is soon trapped in the life of crime forever.

"Remember that there is no 'small theft,'" their mothers had told the two of them; there are small minds; there are small hearts; but there are no small thefts.

"But this child looks famished," said Nonna to herself.

"But this child looks famished," said Nonno to himself, and it could be that their mothers had lied. Nonno followed Nonna around town some more in search of... in search of... that hair that made his heart leap and he followed her closer than before. He said: "She must know that I am behind her; she must know but she never turns around." He said: "She must not know that I am behind her; she must not know but she never turns around." He said to himself: "She has a lover; she has a lover; she has a fiancé; she has a fiancé; she has a husband; she has a husband." But she had none of these and Nonno followed her in circles around town until the sun became pink and then he followed her home.

The two reached the doorsteps of Nonna's father's house and Nonno moved in front of her to open the door for her. Nonno climbed the stairs to pass her and that was when he saw her face for the first time and Nonna's life is said to have started at the moment that Nonno opened the door for her. The pins had helped them: the pin in Nonna's hair (that fastened the rose to the end of the braid and so had lured his attention to her that time that he had found her all alone in the streets and asked her, as she stepped into her father's house, if she would like to be married to him) and also the pin on which the old woman had almost choked to her death (and so had kept Nonna from those delicious fruits that she desired with each side of her heart but which would have deformed the children that she and Nonno would have in the future if she had eaten even one of them).

Nonna hums opera the entire afternoon to me and with pins in her mouth (between her teeth), too. "Nonna," I ask her. "Nonna, aren't you afraid that you will almost choke to death on these pins like that old woman in the fruit stand?" But Nonna has to maintain the notes to "FIGARO... figaro... figaro... FIGARO" and it is a miracle that sometimes Nonna serenades me not with the music alone but with the words, too (the entire time with pins in her mouth).

I ask Nonna to explain to me the words of "La Donna E Mobile" and Nonna responds that adults are as foolish as children are and that she is content to be an old woman and to eat all of the red ripe pomegranates that she wants in peace. I ask her how does she know that she will not have more babies in the future and Nonna tells me that her favorite opera song has been, for as far back as she can remember, "La Donna E Mobile," and the title of this one pulls at the corners of my brain as I attempt to translate it. "*La Donna*... the female ... *E*... is ... *Mobile*... a piece of furniture. The female is a piece of furniture."

I have tried to understand it for centuries now but I still don't know the reason that someone would write music about that and I ask Mamma about it. Mamma chuckles and puts it into order and tells me: " 'Mobile' not like 'furniture' but like 'mobile'... in other words ... 'fickle.' " "The female is fickle" relieves me for a moment, but then I wonder about the reason that someone would write music that said that Nonna and Mamma and I are fickle.

But now Nonna hums to me and it is at the point in the music that Nonna reaches "Mobile" that Nonna tells me once more that her life has amounted to a collection of pins and that Nonno—tossed into a war and then into a prison camp—returned home once and his mother had died and he did not feel like much himself. Nonno had locked himself into a bedroom for weeks and it had been with her hairpins that Nonna had picked the lock of the door in order to force food into Nonno's throat and Nonna had to slide his food underneath the cracks of the bedroom door (as if Nonno were a mouse) like this for months and months because Nonno believed that the Nazis still knocked on the doors of the town for him. But Nonna knocked on the bedroom door for him and remembered the red fruit from the fruit stands and consoled herself with the fact that her first child would not be the scarred toad that it could have been otherwise. The fact is that Nonno had found her on the street that afternoon so that her life could start and children were a start of a definite kind.

Her life is said to have started at the moment that Nonno first admired the braid and followed her home and talked to her father. Nonno married Nonna and he could now touch her hair in the blackness of their own room after Nonna had taken all of the pins out of it and laid it flat over the one pillow that the two of them shared. The red hair had made his life seem worthwhile, all at once, the first time that he had seen it, and then the fact that he had saved the life of an old woman in front of Nonna meant that their married life—their two lives that had been coiled into one life like a French braid—*had* to be worthwhile, after all.

The conflicts of this married life (his parents colder and colder to her and her parents hotter and hotter to him) disappeared as she removed each one of those metal constraints from her hair and unfolded the French braid and came to bed and he often dreamed with his hands in her hair and then he was in medical school and then he was drafted. Il Duce and his papers had told him that it (the Cause) needed his medical services in the war but then Italia had switched sides in the war and the Nazis started to put all of the Italian soldiers (medical or not) into concentration camps for treason. He had cried for two weeks for the feel of her as if he had lost a mother but the third week he crawled into a corner like a ghost: silent and dead. But one time in that corner he felt a stir in his stomach and he arrived home six months later and his relatives prepared to tell him about his mother's death, but he already knew about her death and even the exact time of her death because he had felt it while crouched in that small corner. He then cried for two more weeks and crawled into bed with his wife but then the third week there was that ghost in the corner of the room once more but this time it was a corner in his own bedroom in his own house.

"La Donna E Mobile... " Nonna lilts in the kitchen with the pins still in her hair and tells me that after Nonno returned from the war and sat like a shadow in the corner of the bedroom that there had been so little food in the house for them to eat that she—Nonna—had decided to find work in the factories because she still had months before the child would be born and had no other children in the house to take care of now. "La Donna E Mobile" and I still translate "mobile" into "furniture"—into love seats and couches—in the childish mind that I still have. Nonna explains to me that I've confused the connotation of the words once more and that the woman is not a piece of furniture in the opera but that the woman is fickle.

Nonno had stuck pins into Nonna before she headed for the work at the factories (for her own protection from the menaces of men in the outside world he said to her). Nonno pinned her underwear to her dress so that she could not even urinate the entire time that she was at work.

Mamma tells me that she, too, used to think that the "mobile" in "La Donna E Mobile" meant "mobile" as in "furniture" and not "mobile" as in "fickle." Mamma loves to talk about Latin roots and the Latin root is the same nonetheless for both: both "fickle" and "furniture" are created from an abstract idea about movement, and as furniture can be moved across the floor, a fickle woman can pace across the floor like a piece of mobile furniture.

Nonna had not been able to urinate the entire time that she was at work in the clothes factories and in spite of the fact that Nonna stitched and unstitched fabrics and inserted and removed pins during her ten-hour shift Nonna could not unstitch her own underwear or remove the pins that he had fastened her with. Nonna said that if she needed to use the bathroom it felt like pinpricks in her sides and she realized that it was because woman is fickle and that her boss at work was a man (and not that she is a piece of furniture) that Nonno had insisted that her clothes be fastened in such a method that he could tell if someone else had unpinned her. But because Nonna had eaten no pomegranates the child that she delivered nine months later was born without facial blemishes and it was soon after his birth that Nonna left the factories and that her life became an endless row of baby cloths and diaper pins.

One time Nonno-the-shadow-in-the-bedroom-corner became so ill that he needed a shot but he would not let the doctor touch him so that Nonna had to be the one to take off his pants and to needle him in the behind.

(Nonno never talks about red hair now.)

Nonna has had a life that has been all pins and needles, pins and needles, pins and needles.

It is because of Nonna and the factories that I never use the woods for a toilet. I could not remove the cotton underwear that I wear into the woods if I tried. Either Nonna has hexed all of the underwear that I own to make them refuse to come off in the woods or I must have been conceived at a certain time in the afternoon in which Nonna was still full of pins in her hair and in her mouth and I materialized from the same box of pins as Nonna. The men return from their own relief in the woods (hands still on their belts) but Nonna and I hold it until we are home and then we take hours in the bathroom.

Nonna and Mamma tell me while I am in the bathroom that pins could kill me: I am not even allowed near them except if I am to run down to the store on the corner and purchase a box of them for Nonna. If I am sent to the store with a thousand-lira note and the pins cost eight hundred and fifty lira, then I am allowed to keep the rest. This is because of bad luck: Both Nonna and Mamma believe (and so I am forced to believe too) the hex of the pins: "Pins and other materials with sharp points in them can kill the people whom we love if we are not careful," and so we must never give them as presents to those that we love. No one here would ever think that a set of knives made a nice present for a new bride because the bride would have to either reimburse them for the set of knives or else she would fall ill and die from all of those points and even if Nonna needs to borrow a needle and thread from Mamma then Nonna hands Mamma a coin for the needle.

I have in a drawer a picture of Nonna from the time that she used to work in the factories and the photo is black and white and Nonna does not smile at all but instead she looks like an irritated black bat. To look like a bat must have been popular then and Nonna is smoking a cigarette and is reading a newspaper and not looking at the camera in the least. Her knee is propped up and I am one of the four people in the entire world who can look up her skirt in that picture and see that her underwear has been stitched to her outerwear because her life was all pins even then and because "mobile" means "fickle" and not a piece of furniture, after all.

One time Nonna pricked her hand on a pin and it started to bleed in front of me: I cried for her and remembered what horrible luck it was to have a pin stuck in the palm of the hand, in spite of the fact that pins are useful and hold Nonna's hair in a French chignon now that her hair is not so red as it had been in the times before I was born.

In the times before I was born I don't know who laid Nonna's clothes out for her on a chair in the mornings but in the time after I was born and could match clothes this person has been me. Most of her clothes are blue and sometimes to tease her I call her "the blue MaNonna" because the blue Madonna is the statue of the Madonna that Nonna is fond of the most and she stores it above her dresser so that I can look at it, too. Like the blue Madonna, Nonna wears lots of blue and smells like an old perfumed handkerchief (purple violets). I set Nonna's blue clothes on the chair in her bedroom for her and I can see the holes in the clothes near the "immodest necklines" that Nonna still fastens with old cameo brooches. Nonna is old and can eat all the kinds of fruit that she wants now but she is still careful to fasten her necklines and I can see that her life has landed on pins once more.

I once overheard a conversation I had heard before which stated that Nonna's life started at the moment that Nonno found her red hair on the street and married it. I asked her for the first time, "But Nonna, what about the time before Nonno fell in love with your long, red hair and it was all in a pin . . . but tell me about the time before he fell in love with the hair and married it . . . and tell me about the time before . . . "

But Nonna responds that the events of her life amount to a pile of pins that she has kept in a dresser for the last four decades and that I'll see it soon, too. "Pins." Nonna repeats it in case I have missed her peculiar retort. "Pins." Because woman is fickle (and not a piece of furniture after all, as Mamma and I had been mistaken), all that Nonna's life has consisted of has been an endless stream of stitches and of pins that she stores in a small box in a small dresser drawer and she stores them for Mamma and for me.

Good Luck,
From Patsy
to you.

Patricia Traxler

Here I am at age seven, just coming to terms with my big, new front teeth, but already on comfortable terms with the concept of luck.

Patricia Traxler, whose writing has appeared in such publications as *Ms.*, the *Nation*, the *Kenyon Review*, *Ploughshares*, the *American Voice*, and the *Boston Phoenix Literary Supplement*, was 1990-92 Bunting Poetry Fellow at Radcliffe, and recipient of the 1992 Writers Voice Award for Fiction. Her third collection of poetry, *Forbidden Words*, was recently published by the University of Missouri Press, and she has just completed a novel, *Earthly Luck*, from which this story is taken.

A native Californian, Traxler currently lives in Kansas.

Patricia Traxler

Earthly Luck

It's not the World Out There, I said. It's something smaller, easier to disappear in, not heroic. I was trying to describe my new life.

Do you have many lovers? he asked. Things always get back to sex for Jonathan, I suddenly remembered, which may have been the quality I liked most and least in him when we were married.

We went for a walk by the ocean then, which did not help. But, of course, it's never easy to become reacquainted with a person. Nor with an ocean. In the case of the person, so much has usually changed, so many presences have intruded with the passage of time, that you feel in some way crowded.

And in the case of an ocean, exactly nothing has changed, which allows you to feel as if you have never been gone from it, which only serves to remind you that you have indeed been gone from it. Which makes you feel keenly the loss of it from your life.

But, after all, didn't I choose to leave the ocean five years ago when I fell in love with Will Shanley, who once almost had a play produced for public television, and who lives like a hermit in Dimetown, Nebraska?

Glimmer Train Stories, Issue 11, Summer 1994

And didn't I, for that matter, leave a husband, as well? Whom I loved? And with whom I was now strolling by the ocean?

And didn't I leave a life that allowed me luxuries like silk dresses, health insurance, and good wine? And my days free to pursue my writing?

No, I do not have any lovers at all, I finally said. Mostly I don't think about sex these days. Really.

I could tell he didn't believe me.

I've changed, I told him.

No one could change that much, he answered.

I thought of Will then. Of how he literally took me that first time. I'd always thought the term *took*, as in *he took her swiftly and without sentiment*, was sexist and dumb. But the first time I went to bed with Will he undressed me, then undressed himself, looking me over all the while. I wondered if this was his idea of foreplay. And though I was to discover as time went on what a scholar of every sort of foreplay he was, this first time he simply pushed me back on the bed and *took* me. Never asked about me. Did not show the slightest concern for my pleasure.

And even though I didn't come that first time, it was in some way thrilling. Like being run over by a train in the dark.

That was before he fell in love with one of his students.

That was before my mother, Eileen Sweeney O'Toole, who's never gotten over being Irish, wrote me the first of several letters mentioning *earthly luck*. How we should never give up in our quest for it. No matter how badly we've screwed up our lives. *Earthly luck*, she wrote, *is a horse of many colors*. My mother has a facility for malapropisms.

That was, in fact, three months before I sold the house in San Diego and took the twins out of school, packed us up, shipped our furniture ahead, and moved to Dimetown, Nebraska, where Will told me in short order that, although he realized he'd asked me to move there, seeing me with two thirteen-year-olds to raise and a house to run *took the magic out of it somehow*.

How can I help but see you differently now? is how I believe he put it.

And there I was, in Dimetown, Nebraska.

Why have you stayed there? Jonathan asks over dinner. I mean, *why*?

I didn't want to come back to California with nothing to show for it.

Wouldn't that have been better than staying in Dimetown with nothing to show for it? he inquires, working intently on his sushi.

I watch him, never having understood how people can be logical and eat at the same time. I don't tell him what Alf Brandert, my editor, has said more than once. That I only stay in Dimetown because I hold out hope that someday Will and I might get back together if I stay in the vicinity.

I wouldn't take Will Shanley back, not on a platter, but I find it too embarrassing somehow to tell Alf—or Jonathan—the real reason I can't leave Dimetown: I'm broke ... I haven't the money to leave now that I'm here. There. A fine mess I've gotten myself into. It'd cost a fortune to ship everything home again, and once I scraped up that money, how would I afford San Diego's high-dollar rent and still limit my work to half-time jobs to leave time for my writing?

I figure I've already disgraced myself as a romantic sap anyway, by moving to Dimetown for Will. Why add economic ruin to my list of public embarrassments?

Involuntary exile is way more humiliating than the voluntary kind, no matter what the reason.

I fiddle with my sushi. No way I will tell Jonathan I'm broke. Instead, I tell him that under no circumstances will I consider eating the raw quail egg before me, though I will be happy to eat the salmon eggs that form a bed beneath it.

You still haven't got used to sushi, he says.

In Dimetown? Remember, Jonathan, I don't live in California anymore. There isn't a sushi bar on every street corner in Dimetown. And, anyway, what's so hot about sushi? A lot of things about So Cal make me laugh, now that I'm away from it all, I add.

Sushi isn't California cuisine, it's *Japanese*, he says, as if he were talking to a wheat farmer who'd just stepped down off the combine to ask for dining information.

Whatever, I tell him.

And, anyway, he says, what's this *California* thing? You're a native Californian, remember? Could it be you've absorbed a bit of that provincial heartland attitude toward the Coast?

I bite my tongue to avoid saying how much I hate hearing people refer to it as *the Coast*, as if it were the only one. Coast, I mean. Instead, I just grin at him and say, Well, at least you don't wear gold chains around your neck and a pinky ring. Yet.

Don't insult me, he says.

We sit quietly for a while, chewing and thinking.

I blame myself for our breakup, he tells me.

It wasn't your fault.

You stopped loving me, he says.

We both know that isn't true. In the least. But we are both silent for a time.

I lost faith, I finally tell him. Someone else touched me in a way that gave me new faith, so I left, but then he didn't meet my train. The kids and I got off the Amtrak in Obart, Nebraska, at three in the morning and no one was there. We walked down the pale, dusty main street of town, and no one was anywhere. Nothing was open. We saw a blue light flickering in a window down the block. We walked to it with our suitcases bulging, the twins in front of me on the sidewalk. The Nebraska winter cold was sharp and unfamiliar against our faces. The sight of Andy's ears bent outward from his knit cap, like pearlescent handles, filled me with dumb grief. Inside the storefront with blue lights, we found a fat couple: the man was wearing a sleeveless undershirt and some oil-stained green polyester slacks. The woman had on a gaping chenille robe. Her red hair had gray roots and was held back by black bobby pins. I hadn't seen bobby pins in anyone's hair since I was a kid. The blue light flickering was their black-and-white TV. They had a small cab service. Always waited up, it seems, for the three-o'clock train. The windup clock on the man's TV tray said 3:11. His name was Mervil Shank.

Jonathan has paused over his sushi. That sounds kind of appealing, really, he says. Walking down the sidewalk, I mean, of a one-street Midwest town at three a.m.

He says it as if what I'd described contained some sort of Real-Life ambience. Southern Californians often pine for that.

You think it sounds good, eh? I look at him. He pops a quail egg into his mouth. Well, that's easy for you to say, I mutter.

Mwrrf, he says.

Don't insult me, I answer.

How's your writing coming along?

I write nearly every day.

But are you sending it out?

No.

What does your pal in New York say about that?

What does any editor say about that? He says if I don't get the book to him soon, I can forget it. But I know he doesn't mean it.

What about magazines? Are you sending things to them?

No.

I sigh, look out at the ocean. *Earthly luck,* my mother wrote in a recent letter, *is there for all of us. But sometimes we don't know it when we see it. When that happens, we have only ourselves to blame.* My mother is fond of pointing out things like that.

I look at the springy red hairs on Jonathan's wrists. It's easy to remember why I've always loved him, though I mustn't let myself forget that Jonathan can be a difficult man.

He is the only man I've ever known who cared about my work.

Let me revise that: he is the only man I've ever slept with who cared about my work.

Most men I've met are incapable of doing both with the same woman.

Will's mother, Myrtle, told me once, *The problem with your relationship is that both you and Will are full of devotion and concern—for Will.*

She was right and I resented her for it.

How long will you be in California? he asks me.

I can only stay a few days, I say. Just to get the kids set for college. I have to avoid his eyes because that is a lie. I could stay for two months if I wanted. But then I wouldn't be able to bear going back to Dimetown. And I have a contract with the Nebraska State Arts Council. To teach poetry writing to the blind. Starting in October, which is two months away. In Dimetown and surrounding counties.

I wish you could stay longer, he says. I look at his hairy wrists.

So do I.

He puts his arms around me and I can hear the ocean behind the pounding sound that is either in his chest or in my skull. It's easy to remember why I've always loved him. Beyond his wrists and my work.

I don't want to be someone you have to tell Clare about, I tell him. Clare is the woman he lives with now. When she isn't bobbing noses in San Francisco.

I have no intention of talking to Clare about us. This thing with you and me—it was before her, before everything.

Well, I don't want to be someone you *don't* tell her about, either.

He sighs.

Obart, Nebraska, is about seventy miles away from Dimetown, but it is the nearest Amtrak stop. We had Mervil Shank drive us to the Obartian Arms, which looked like a Holiday Inn gone bad. The twins slept fine, as kids often do, Andy on his stomach, his face crushed into the pillow, mouth open in an astonished sort of way, Bird snoozing on her back, arms up as if a holdup victim, the front of her T-shirt sporting the legend *Toto, where the hell are we?*, which inexplicably caused my eyes to well up a little.

I sat up and smoked till five-thirty, a half-full pack of Parliaments I found in the bedstand. I don't smoke, wasn't sure how to, had last smoked a cigarette when I was fourteen and wanted to be cool, but I smoked every cigarette, as if changing one long-standing truth about myself might help me to accommodate other personal changes more difficult and of obscure, still undisclosed necessity.

Obartian, I thought. What have I done to my children.

He'd asked me, begged me, to move to Nebraska so we could be together. *Once a man has found a woman who understands his jokes, pleases his eye, replaces his muse—and satisfies fantasies he didn't even know he had—life stalls,* Will had written me, *and he can't go on unless he has her with him.*

That was easy for him to say. A lot of things are easy for people to say, I've noticed, and those are the things I try not to believe. These days.

After dinner, we drove to the Del Mar beach house Jonathan took after our divorce and which he still keeps, although he and Clare often stay at her La Jolla place when she's in town.

Clare is a plastic surgeon, who divides her time between San Diego and San Francisco. Jonathan is a psychologist-turned-entrepreneur, who divides his time between Los Angeles and San Diego. I teach poetry writing to the blind in Dimetown, Nebraska. And surrounding counties.

But I still have the silk dresses which I do not wear, having no place to wear them in Dimetown.

I do not still have the good wine, having long since guzzled it.

I do not have the group health insurance, since I do not belong to a group.

Nor do I still have the free time to pursue my writing as I used to.

Nor do I still have my kids with me, having helped them to relocate to their father's place in Orange County because they can attend a good college more affordably in California than is possible in Nebraska. And they can reestablish connections with relatives and friends they haven't had a chance to spend time with in five years. That's always been our plan. And of course they are almost eighteen, an age when lots of kids move away to go to school.

And I will stay on in Dimetown, Nebraska, where I know I can afford to live without working so many hours that I haven't any time at all to write. And I will teach poetry writing to the blind, half-time.

And my second husband is walking beside me near the ocean. My ex-second husband. Sounds pretty Southern California I know, but it never seemed so in reality.

The kids' father, my first husband, is a fire chief who wears sweatpants at every possible moment of his life. And who once, in a restaurant of his choice—I believe it was called the Raging Bull—told me that I could not order the baked potato with my steak because it cost extra. And who then ordered himself a baked potato, saying that he was larger than I and needed it more.

Then I married Jonathan, who is now walking beside me near the ocean, which doesn't help at all, and whom I have always loved, although I finally left him in a lapse of faith and ran off to Dimetown, Nebraska, to be with a hermit who tired of me in seven months and fell in love with one of his students, a girl of nineteen who thought white bread was elegant and whole-wheat, ethnic. And who had once confided in me her "philosophy of makeup."

Am I making all this sound as if I never really loved Will? Because, if I am, it's not true. I loved him. My mother says I was addicted to him. I realize the two statements are not the same, but I imagine both were true. The thing is, it's never easy to explain love or addiction.

Her philosophy of makeup was that one should wear it at all times, including to bed at night, because otherwise she would have two different faces, one for daytime and one for night. And that would be phony, she told me, to have two different faces. I can't stand anything phony, she added.

I think you should come into my bedroom, Jonathan says, and I think to myself, Sure, *your* bedroom—though she undoubtedly sleeps there with you fairly regularly and has two or three sheer nightgowns hanging in the closet. But I say nothing except to ask if I can use the bathroom and he says yes. I go past the one in the hall and toward the one that must be in the master bedroom, remembering that he has said there are two bathrooms in his town house at the beach.

Wait, he says, there's a bathroom off the hall—you just walked past it.

That's okay, I reassure him. And I keep walking.

Sure enough, some black cotton DKNY tights are there, same size I wear, hung to dry, and a terrific pair of baggy black cotton pants by Issey Miyake. Next to them, hanging over the towel bar, is a washed silk shirt—the roomy kind of shirt I love—in a sort of Mondrian-looking magenta, black, and yellow geometric print. I look at the label: Giorgio Armani. That's when I know I can't go to bed with Jonathan. Before I leave the bathroom, I spray some of her Opium perfume on, just to mess with his mind.

When the kids and I got to Dimetown, which we accomplished early the next day by asking Mervil Shank to drive us the entire seventy miles in his taxi (and which cost just forty-seven dollars), we went straight to Will's house. (Wait till you meet him, I told them. We've talked to him on the phone a jillion times, Bridget answered. Yeah, we already know him, said Andrew. Yes, but he's much better in person, I told them confidently as I rapped on his front door.)

He wasn't home. Wasn't home, though he'd told me that the day I was due in would be so red-letter that he wouldn't think of leaving his house for even a minute. That was, in case he'd been unable to drive to Obart and pick us up at the depot. Which he apparently had been. Unable.

So we had Mervil Shank, the Obartian cabbie, drive us to the Dimetown Hilton. Which I later learned was being enjoined by the Hilton Hotel chain to stop using their name. It seemed that Harley Dean Hilton, local Dimetown hotelier, could not see where he was in the wrong for using his own name (above the official Hilton Hotel logo). The Dimetown Hilton became, in time, the Dimetown Hillside Inn, though there was not a hill for a hundred miles in any direction.

I can't possibly sleep with you now, I tell him.

Why? What do you mean *now*?

I've seen her clothes. Somehow it makes a difference. Now I perceive her as real. A little hung up on name designers, but real, in a way, all the same.

I don't want to hurt you, he says. If it would hurt you, let's forget it.

I hate him for saying that. Even though it's true that I can't sleep with him now anyway. Having seen her clothes.

I love you for that, I tell him. Really.

How about some Chet Baker? he suggests. He remembers that Chet is my favorite.

I'd prefer Mozart, I tell him. Or Willie Nelson. I'm punishing him.

Sure, he obliges, and puts on *The Magic Flute*. What else, I think sarcastically.

I close my eyes, imagine Clare as Queen of the Night. Somehow it helps.

He takes me in his arms again and says, Let's just lie close together—I understand about the rest. I look at his wrists and my eyes fill up. I look down so he won't see, and that causes some tears to fall onto his right hand. He kindly pretends not to notice. But I know him better than that.

I know him better than anything.

Which doesn't help.

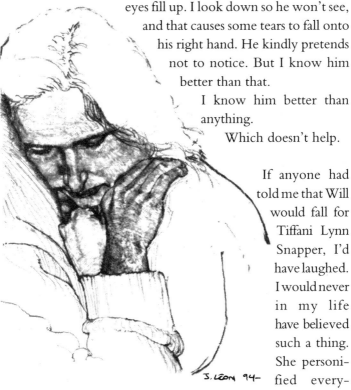

If anyone had told me that Will would fall for Tiffani Lynn Snapper, I'd have laughed. I would never in my life have believed such a thing. She personified everything he claimed to despise in a female: artificiality (she wore *eye shadow* beneath her cheekbones!), superficiality, giddiness, vanity. (Okay, maybe he regularly made exceptions for vanity, I can't be a complete hypocrite. And I have to admit that behind the gaudy makeup, her skin was like a Botticelli. A nineteen-year-old flame-haired Botticelli.) When she had the lead in the spring play at the college, soon after I arrived in Dimetown, I'd gotten to know her (as far as one can get to know someone like that) because Will had called upon me to design the sets. So she knew all about Will and me. Knew I'd moved to Dimetown to be with him.

And I realized much too late that her awareness of that—my moving there to be with him—had made him more interesting in her eyes. I remember the day when she and I were backstage, as she waited for rehearsal to begin, and she asked me why in the world I'd ever moved to Dimetown in the first place.

I'd give *anything* to live where you moved from, she said. Southern California is my ideal place to live. Someday I'm going to go there to act or be a cosmetologist. What did you do there? Are you an actress?

I wrote, I said. Worked for Norman Lear for a few years, doing script consultation for some Tandem shows that had begun to slide a little in the ratings, like "All in the Family" and "Maude." Sold a couple of pilots, too. But I consider poetry my real work, and I can do that anywhere.

But you don't get a lot of money for poetry, do you?

No, poets and playwrights rarely get rich. I'm sure Will would tell you that, I added, warming as I looked over to where he was standing as he coached the male lead. Which is why, I told her, I'm going to have to find some teaching.

But why in the world did you ever move to a dead little place like this?

I thought you knew why, I said.

No. Why?

To be with Will.

Will? she said incredulously, and I could see her looking over toward him, no doubt appraising his worn jacket and tattered jeans. You moved here to be with Will?

Yeah. We needed to be together. It's pretty hard being passionately in love from half a continent away.

Her eyes—there's no other way I can say it—widened. She looked over once again to where he was standing, and I began wishing I hadn't said *passionately*. There was curiosity all over her face.

We get up from the couch and go for another walk by the ocean.

It's hard to believe you're thirty-seven, he says. You look about twenty-five. Twenty-seven, at most.

Thirty-six, I say.

What?

I'm thirty-six.

Well, whatever. You look even younger than you did when you left five years ago.

It's possible, I think to myself; things had become pretty tense toward the end. But what good is it to look twenty-five or twenty-seven? Why can't I look nineteen? Maybe then things would be different. I despise myself for allowing such a thought to enter my highly evolved head. I know better, and I know it.

I blame myself for your leaving, he says. If I'd given you the affection and support you deserved, you'd never have gone.

That's easy for you to say, I smile. And I kiss his neck.

Was it good with him?

Yes.

Were you tired of me?

No.

Yes you were.

No. I was never tired of you. It's just that something happened. I lost faith in us. And then I met him. I can't describe it. But I never stopped caring about you.

Don't tell me you didn't love him, because I won't believe you.

I'm not telling you that.

I found out eventually that Will had told everyone who asked that he *didn't know why* I had moved to Dimetown. *You'd have to ask her about that*, they told me he'd said. *I have no idea*, he told them. *How should I know why she moved here?*

Which, of course, gave them all the idea that he was some kind of romantic god and I was some pathetic groupie, enamored of the man who'd written *Buffalo Gothic* and almost had it produced for public television. Because, by that time, a lot of people also knew what I'd told Tiffani Lynn. That I'd moved to Dimetown to be with Will.

I have never felt so betrayed.

I kick off my shoes and walk toward the water. Jonathan doesn't ask where I'm going. That's one thing I like about Jonathan. He doesn't ask you about everything you do. Unlike me.

Before I reach the water, I pull up my skirt and remove my new shimmertights, throw them in the sand. I run then, keep running until I'm in the surf, my wet dress holding my body the way plastic wrap hugs cheese. I just want to be inside all this movement, oblivious to everything outside it. *Whoopee*, I say softly, in order to relieve the moment of any lurking drama. *Wahoo.*

Life is full of signs, my mother has said, but usually we are not smart enough to respect them as we should. That, or we want something enough that we don't *want* to read the signs. Like the day in the Dimetown New World Laundromat when Will told me that he'd never felt he'd had his share of women. His *share.*

I nearly dropped the blouse I was folding, watched him continue his own folding as if he'd said nothing unusual. Never had his what? Of what? I thought we were madly in love. I reached into the basket for a washcloth to fold and said, not knowing what else to say, Well, how many have you had?

Oh, somewhere in the teens, he answered, looking a little startled. I didn't usually ask him about his past, and my question probably surprised us both too much for either of us to stop and question it. But upon further consideration, it seemed to me that, if he'd brought it up, he was asking for it.

Then came his question, which I hadn't expected. Although I knew that I, too, had asked for it.

How many men have you been with? I thought it was funny the way he referred to *having* women, but *being with* men.

Three, I answered. I was embarrassed by the dearth, but what was the point in lying?

Counting me?

Yeah.

And the other two were your husbands.

Obviously, yes.

Well, Will said after a moment, that's plenty for a woman.

Now, I agreed that three was plenty for me, since I was so satisfied with Will sexually, but I had to fold three towels before I could stop shaking with simple indignation—at least I was pretty sure that was what it was—that he considered three *plenty* for me, while at the same time considering *somewhere in the teens* to be less than his *share.*

I miss clotheslines, I said then, and I think fabric softeners are so false. I turned to him amid the sounds of tumbling laundry. And, I told him, I don't know what you're talking about.

Honey, he said, you're rambling again. And then he put his arm around me, gave me a squeeze and added, But you have a marvelous ass.

Sure, I told him. But what about my line-breakage?

I knew he thought I was kidding. Still I waited to see if he would answer.

This is not the World Out There. It's something smaller, easy to disappear in, not heroic.

The flight back was rough. We had to circle Stapleton for thirty minutes due to turbulent weather. My connecting flight, which came into Denver from Portland and would carry me to Omaha, was an hour late.

I think it hurt Jonathan that I wouldn't sleep with him. How could I explain all the reasons? The more reasons you give for something, the more false you sound. André Gide once said, *One cannot be sincere and at the same time seem so.*

By the time I'd driven from Omaha to Dimetown, a two-hour drive, I was practically hallucinating from exhaustion.

The house was, of course, exactly as I'd left it. I didn't go into the kids' rooms, but I went through the rest of the house, room to room, greeting plants and furniture with a kind of quiet pleasure. I thought of all the people in the world, including myself, about whom my mother could have said, *They have only themselves to blame.*

I thought about that for a while, and I knew there was no one else I wanted to blame.

Your life would go on just as always, I'd told Jonathan. Imagining he might say, *What? Go on as always? How could my life go on as always once we'd made love again after five years?* It's true neither of us would ever go back to the other now. Still, I guess I was wishing to hear him say that making love with me again would change his life somehow.

Instead he simply said, That's true.

That's easy for you to say, I told him. You don't live a celibate life in Dimetown, Nebraska.

You're shivering, he told me. You shouldn't have run into the ocean at night with all your clothes on.

The ocean is the only thing in my life that hasn't changed, I told him. And, I thought, I'd take an ocean over a person any day. Myself included.

I love you, I said.
I've always loved you, he answered quietly.

When we hit a spot of turbulence just before landing in Omaha, I happened to look around the plane at all the faces nearby. As the plane rocked and drifted, you could see it in the jaws, almost to a one, the tensing and straining to get us down past that last small expanse of sky. All those faces, like my own, straining toward earthly luck.

ABDELRAHMAN MUNIF

Mixing it up with oil, politics, and fiction

Interview

by Michael Upchurch

Like Paul Scott's Raj Quartet, *Arab writer Abdelrahman Munif's oil trilogy (*Cities of Salt, The Trench, Variations on Night and Day*) attempts to squeeze a whole country at a pivotal period in its history into the liberating confines of fiction. The country, in Munif's case, is a Persian Gulf kingdom bearing a close resemblance to his native Saudi Arabia, and the history encompasses a period from the 1920s to the 1950s, when the autocratic regime of Mooran (as Munif calls it) consolidates its hold on the Arabian peninsula, taps into vast oil reserves with Western help, and changes the lives of its nomadic and oasis tribal citizens irretrievably.*

photo credit Intishal Kadhim

Abdelrahman Munif

It is a breathtakingly ambitious project and one which Munif is uniquely qualified to take on. Born circa 1933 into a Saudi Arabian trading family, he was raised in Jordan and received his higher education in Baghdad, Cairo, and Belgrade, where he earned his Ph.D. in oil economics. He went on to work as director of crude-oil marketing for the Syrian Oil Company and as editor-in-chief of Oil and Development, *a Baghdad monthly periodical.*

Glimmer Train Stories, Issue 11, Summer 1994

For three decades he has been a writer in exile, incurring the displeasure of the Saudi Arabian regime, first for his political views and later for his fiction. For a time he lived in France, where he wrote the trilogy's first volume, Cities of Salt. *He now lives in Damascus with his Syrian wife, Suad, with whom he has four children.*

His books reflect the striking variety of his life. Cities of Salt, *which opens in the 1930s with a glimpse of the oasis settlement of Wadi al-Uyoun ("an outpouring of green amid the harsh, obdurate desert"), examines the plight of the wadi's humble citizens as they uncomprehendingly watch the transformation of their surroundings into a landscape of oil wells and then are shunted off to work in the refinery city of Harran. Munif weaves a wide-ranging tapestry of laborers, traders, middlemen, buffoonish emirs, and inscrutable Americans, all of them haunted by a fierce family patriarch, Miteb al-Hathal, who refuses to accept the changes in his world and withdraws into the desert. The rumors and sightings of him there lend an almost supernatural cast to the novel.*

The Trench *takes the action up to the 1950s and moves in closer to Mooran's rulers, Sultan Khazael and his half-brother Fanar, seeing them mostly through the eyes of social climber Dr. Subhi Mahmilji and his unhappily adulterous wife, Widad. The latest volume,* Variations on Night and Day, *moves back in time to the 1920s to offer a scathing yet fascinating portrait of Khazael and Fanar's father, Sultan Khureybit, whom readers will be tempted to see as real-life Saudi ruler King Abdul-Aziz ibn Saud, the canny warrior who united most of the Arabian peninsula into one country. The glimpses Munif provides of harem politics and of a British diplomat-schemer, known simply as Hamilton, add to the intricate mix of power play and vendetta.*

In person, Munif is a dapper man who combines an air of intensity with a ready sense of humor. While he understands English with relative ease, he felt more comfortable giving his answers in Arabic. This interview was held during Munif's second U.S. visit (to take part in Seattle's 1993 Bumbershoot Arts Festival) and was conducted with the help of Peter Theroux, the gifted American translator of the trilogy, and Hanna Eady, a Palestinian theater producer living in Seattle. I am indebted to them for their valiant simultaneous translation efforts, and especially to Peter Theroux who took the time afterward to listen through the tape recording of the interview and offer corrections and clarifications.

UPCHURCH: *The* Cities of Salt *trilogy is a vast project to take on, grand in scale and ambition. Yet you wrote it quite quickly, in less than ten years. When did you first conceive it? Was there a particular moment when you said, "Yes, this is my work. This is what I've got to do"?*

MUNIF: The actual writing process didn't take very long, from about 1981 until 1989, but the preparation for it and the thought given to it went on much longer. Being from that region and having had a long career in oil, the writing of a novel concerned with oil was a project that was on my mind for some time—especially because I had dealt with it in a previous novel, *Long Distance Races*, which was an attempt to look at the question of oil as it related to the American-British rivalry in Iran.

That novel showed me that it could be done. However, I thought it could be done again, using the oil topic as a way of getting into the deeper subject matter of the region's history.

On the dust jackets of your books, some of your biographical details are vague—and the novels themselves engender great curiosity about your life. One question raised by Cities of Salt *is whether there is a Wadi al-Uyoun in your own life or the life of your family?*

In our country there are a lot of place-names that are similar to one another. For example, I am from a region called al-Uyoun. But that doesn't mean that there's a complete identification of the place in the book with the place that I knew in my life. Sometimes the novelist chooses a place that is more suitable as a site to be used in a novel—although sometimes the novel imposes its own choice.

You were born into a trading family of Saudi Arabian origin. How was your childhood spent? Was there a lot of traveling?

One of the stranger occurrences in my life is that my father married my mother in Damascus, where I now live. But I was born in Jordan, in Amman. Many families like ours did a lot of traveling and moving around. In my infancy and youth, it was a common and easy thing to go and see the relatives in Saudi Arabia and for the relatives in Saudi Arabia to come and see us. But, four years after my birth, my father died in Amman. While some of our family went back to Saudi Arabia, I stayed in Amman.

One of the reasons for my staying there was school. At that time, education in Saudi Arabia was not always available or easy to find. After finishing high school in 1952, I entered on a period of travel which has lasted until now, so that I have lived in many Arab countries and in many foreign countries. Traveling and leaving countries has become part of my being and life.

What trade was your father in?

Trade is a big word—and the bedouin were small traders. It was not a big and grand commercial enterprise. When a bedouin had gathered together some money, he would buy a camel, he would buy some goods, he would go from place to place and sell them. The sense of what constitutes a merchant or a trader here is different from what makes a trader there. Wandering traders were a common phenomenon.

Did your family usually travel with your father?

At a certain time, yes. For example, when we were young, we brought flour from Amman to Saudi Arabia and, at the same time, brought salt and dates from Saudi Arabia back to Jordan. This was the specific kind of trade that I did in my youth. The first novel I wrote, published in 1973, was entitled *The Trees and the Assassination of Marzuk*, and the protagonist in that book was a wandering trader or peddler named Marzuk.

Unlike many writers, you've had a career in the oil industry, and the oil industry is not noted for producing novelists. How did you choose that career? You came from a small trading family. At some point you must have realized there was this big corporate world out there and you must have made a decision to enter it. What was going through your mind?

I don't have a complete answer for that. At a young age I was a very good reader, and it seemed to me that novel writing was a horizon in which I was interested and which I could reach. Gradually, as other horizons were closed off—and since I didn't have very much interest in being an employee in a larger context—I tried novel writing. So, I imagine, it really was my first choice.

When I was editor-in-chief of the magazine *Oil and Development*, in Baghdad, I told my employers that you could find at least fifty other people who could be editors-in-chief of the magazine, doing what I did—but you couldn't find fifty novelists. And it was my wish to persevere and to pursue the novel writing. Of course, I think it's part of the mission of any artist, no matter what kind, not only to depend on his gift, but to depend on himself and on hard work. If he has a gift, if it *is* there, he can improve it with effort, enlarge it, and build upon it.

What connection did working in the oil industry have with your writing gift?

There is, in our country, a punishment of being an employee without actual employment. It was my punishment. After having spent nearly two years in this shaming condition, of being an employee without work, there was this gap for which I thought the novel might be a solution. We have a saying: In love or other matters, it's like smoking—it starts as a game or flirtation and ends up as an addiction. When I had written my first novel, I had the feeling that this may have been the right path after all, and that I could continue doing this.

Your politics as a young man were nationalist and socialist, while the oil industry has always been notoriously capitalist and antinationalist, simply going wherever the oil is and wherever people need the oil products. It doesn't seem a happy match.

In *Long Distance Races*, I think this is dealt with completely, in the sense that you see the scale of exploitation. It wasn't so much a question of right or left, of socialism or capitalism, but more specifically of our country or region—nothing more absolute or ideological than that. When King Abdul-Aziz ibn Saud decided to grant oil concessions to the Americans, what he got didn't reflect the real worth of the oil. And, of course, our oil resources in the Arab countries are being exploited unjustly. There is an unfair division of it between unequal sides.

On top of that, we find that our share, our country's share, goes to sheiks and princes instead of to the people, and we feel wronged because this is really our one resource. This is our chance to use it to build a country that has something to do with these times. Unfortunately, over the last fifty years, all of this money has been spent wrongly and it means that these countries may soon be living through difficulties that cannot be imagined.

A person who loved his country and who loved his people would try to use this wealth to build a material base to provide for a future. But it is now clear that Saudi Arabia may have used up all of its oil reserves and ended up on the brink of bankruptcy as a result of its misguided oil policies. In other countries where there is oil, it has become part of a comprehensive means of building the country. There should be some more logical way of having this relationship between oil-producing countries and oil-using countries, or of using the oil revenues sensibly.

In most Arab countries, your fiction has been banned. Your books are published in Beirut. You've lived in Syria, Egypt, Iraq, Belgrade, and other places—a very confusing situation for a writer. What audience do you have in mind?

For Arab writers, especially for someone like me, I'm aiming at Arab readers throughout the region. I'm certainly not just aiming at Syria or Iraq or Saudi Arabia. As for the other thing: in our country a banned book is the most widely read book, which shows that it is not easy to restrict or confine a book. From what I know and what I hear, one of the more common gifts among Saudis and their friends are banned books—and particularly my books.

So a novelist has a wide field in front of him in which to work, with the assumption that it's impossible, on the part of leaders, to prevent a reader from reaching the book. It's stupid of them to think such things, especially now with all of the means of communication and ways of transmitting ideas in this age. For example, the memorandum [concerning human-rights abuses in Saudi Arabia] that I sent to the Conference on Human Rights in Vienna [in summer of 1993] was one of the most widely circulated documents of these times in Saudi Arabia. But I wasn't the one doing the work—it was the fax machine! It's like a bird; it's like a plane. There's no confining or restricting it.

When I first came across your work I was under the impression that it was the publication of the books that had led to your losing your Saudi citizenship, but I have since been corrected. What were the circumstances that led to your Saudi citizenship being taken away from you?

You have to understand that our country is different from other countries. The only right that you have there is to support the great leader. Any point of view or remark is a departure from the mainstream. So when I began engaging in political thought, forming certain relationships, using my own reasoning to question the use of our resources or the nature of the regime or the ruling family, they were angered. It ended with the withdrawal of my citizenship. But they pretended that it was only the novel that was a problem and that led to the lifting of my citizenship.

When did this occur?

In 1963. There was a ten-year lag between the lifting of my citizenship and the publication of my first novel in 1973.

So they knew you were writing a novel?

I don't know. The novel, when it appeared, simply became a pretext, an excuse, for actions taken ten years earlier.

Volume one in the trilogy, Cities of Salt, *focuses on the man in the street—or, as it were, the man in the oasis.* The Trench *is more about the social climbers, the people trying to realize ambitions in a changing situation.* Variations on Night and Day, *going back to an earlier time, takes place much more inside the court, dealing directly with the powers that be. I understand that there are two new novels in the series awaiting translation, yet the trilogy as it stands seems very complete to me. How do these two new novels complete or add to the shape of the trilogy?*

While the third novel in the series may more or less complete the circle, there was still in the second volume the beginning of a struggle between the brothers, Prince Fanar and Sultan Khazael, which led to one brother deposing the other.

The fourth novel deals with the Sultan Khazael in exile: his sufferings and disappointments, his bitterness. Yet it all happened to him because he was wrong in his treatment of the people. The fourth novel covers this phase and opens the way for a look at how the victorious brother, Fanar, also became a victim of events and of the mistakes that he made. The cycle of blood and vengeance is never-ending. So the fifth novel deals with how the person who, in the end, was triumphant also became the victim.

I don't think that this novelistic process has an end. I like to leave it open to the reader to think on ahead to what is going to happen.

One thing I've been wondering since the end of Cities of Salt *is when Miteb al-Hathal will come back in from the desert.*

Everyone asks me that, and I always give the same specific response. Miteb al-Hathal is the hero of bygone times. There is no need for him to return. If he came back it would be as a poor, miserable man. For him to remain a phantom or a conscience is the best role for him, because he's incapable of providing a solution to the future.

Cities of Salt *draws very much on experiences which anyone living in Saudi Arabia would have access to. I assume that the village of Wadi al-Uyoun, the oil-refinery city of Harran, and even the court of Harran's local emir are worlds that an ordinary citizen could penetrate and know from experience.*

But The Trench *and* Variations on Night and Day *are much more insider's books. What are your sources for them? Did you research documents about the powers that be, or did your information come from more informal hearsay? What connections did you have with your subject matter?*

Any novel, especially a novel like *Cities of Salt*, depends on a large amount of information from diverse sources. From my connections with the times, the places, the country, and the people who made it, I got much of the detail used in the books. But of course there is a lot of work of the imagination that goes into this becoming an artistic work.

Then again, there are events which I did not experience firsthand, but which other people experienced, that would provide material for novels far more provocative than *Cities of Salt*.

In Peter Theroux's memoir, Sandstorms: Days and Nights in Arabia, *you describe your novels to Theroux as a "parallel history." How freely did you draw on Saudi history in creating the history of Mooran? Did you give yourself any ground rules to follow? And what exactly do you mean by "parallel history"?*

A novel is a complete world encompassing things that have happened and things that could happen, plus the imagination. So when I did sit down to write *Cities of Salt*, it may have been as a novel parallel to this political history, but it was not my intention to write an actual political history. In a case like this, the character in the novel may have a much richer personality than the person who did actually pass through history. One does not want to hold a novelist to the logic that would govern a political historian. Of course, sometimes when there's a topic that I can't write as a novel, I write it as an article in the newspaper, as an analysis, or some other way.

I would prefer that people deal with me and approach me as a novelist rather than as an historian. If the novel intersects with history, that's something that happens in many novels. But unfortunately, people tend to oversimplify. It sometimes bothers me when someone says, for example, that the character of Dr. Subhi Mahmilji is a real-life person, like Rashad Pharaon [a Syrian medical doctor who moved to Saudi Arabia and became a close and trusted adviser to ibn Saud]. Of course, I'm not letting Pharaon off the hook! But because Mahmilji has so much more to him, he is a bigger and richer asset to the book.

I wasn't surprised to see you using a passage from Chekhov as an epigraph in Variations on Night and Day, *but I was almost shocked to see you using one from Anaïs Nin. She strikes me as a writer who explores herself almost to the exclusion of the outside world, while you seem the very opposite. What Western literature has had an effect on you? Who are your influences? Was there any one writer who helped you find your way?*

In public debates, I always say the same thing: A writer should always read a lot—and forget a lot. If he's unable to do that, he will become a prisoner of a certain writer or a certain style.

Of course, if I'm asked about the writers whom I've read with interest or with love, there are a great many of them. I don't want to give you a long list, but for example there's Faulkner—I like him a lot. Dostoevsky: I love him to the same extent that I'm afraid of him. Tolstoy's the same.

We Arab writers have to do this reading, but at the same time create the character of the Arab novel, taking into consideration our countries and our circumstances.

Where did you first encounter writers like Faulkner or Dostoevsky?

It was an important characteristic of the generation of the 1950s that we conceived of politics as an intellectual activity. The way to do that, to become one of the intellectuals who were mainly interested in politics, was to go to the theater and read poetry and novels and educate yourself. It was a kind of culturalization. I was one of those who, at a certain time, especially in Cairo at the end of the 1950s, was always trying to get my friends to read nonpolitical writing. And of course Cairo in the late fifties was a busy time in terms of theater, books, translation, literature. There are certain times that are more fertile than others.

In The Trench *there is great sympathy for and surprising sexual frankness concerning Widad, Dr. Mahmilji's wife. I didn't expect to find adultery and sexuality treated so explicitly in an Arab novel. Was that a contributing factor to the book being banned? Is there a censorship to do with sexual matters?*

If you were to be familiar with Arabic literature of the past, you would realize that there is an absolutely unlimited amount of sex in it! Only fear, on the part of the fundamentalists, has prevented them from trying to ban these books. The last attempt was about four years ago, when there was a new edition of *Thousand and One Nights* which the religious authorities wanted to ban. I push myself and urge others to have the courage to deal with not only politics freely, but also sex.

As for Widad in *The Trench*, I don't think they would have considered that sufficient reason to ban the book. It was other aspects of it that angered them more. In Arabic literature now, particularly the novel, you'll find that people are dealing with sex and other adult concerns more frequently. They're beginning to.

It's easy to see why The Trench *and* Variations *would have offended the political authorities. But with* Cities of Salt, *it isn't so obvious. There is the foolish emir, but he's a local power, not a member of the royal family. Am I missing something?*

Even there, the emir was portrayed in a realistic manner. The rulers always want to give people the impression that they're noble, that they're courageous, and that they're beneficial, humanitarian. And you may not go into an emir's bedroom! When you've entered there, you're on forbidden ground.

In Variations, *you seem to have quite a bit of sympathy for Hamilton, and several things he says read like a credo that might be close to your own: about being on this earth to serve people, about the value of knowledge, about books being the one thing that can gather men together and make them better thinkers. In one conversation he argues, as I imagine you might, that "one of historians' greatest mistakes is to strip history of its spirit, of the place where it transpired, of the people who were part of that history."*

Surely it's ironic, in the context of the trilogy, that you would choose an Englishman to represent such a point of view. Do you feel close to Hamilton? Or are you using him the way Shakespeare uses Polonius, to put wise words in the mouth of an ambivalent or misguided character?

The question of Hamilton is not merely a question of a mouthpiece. He's a man who has an important role in nation building.

There is a famous story told about Muhammad Ali Pasha [an Ottoman ruler of Egypt in the early nineteenth century] who heard of a book in which there were a lot of things that he must have translated so he could read them. The book was *The Prince* by Machiavelli, and every time they translated a chapter, he read it. And when they had finished translating about one-quarter of the book, he said, "That's enough. I know it all already."

It's true that a book can give you information, but life with its diversity and variety gives you so much more. There is in *Variations* a bit of dialogue between Fanar and Hamilton where Fanar *is* The Prince, but with a bedouin mind and in bedouin clothes.

As for using a mouthpiece in the manner of Shakespeare, there are some things that need to be said, no matter who is saying them. You have to know, when reading a novel, that you can't trust the novelist—that he's cunning, that he's wily.

MICHAEL UPCHURCH is a Seattle writer whose novels include *Air* and *The Flame Forest.*

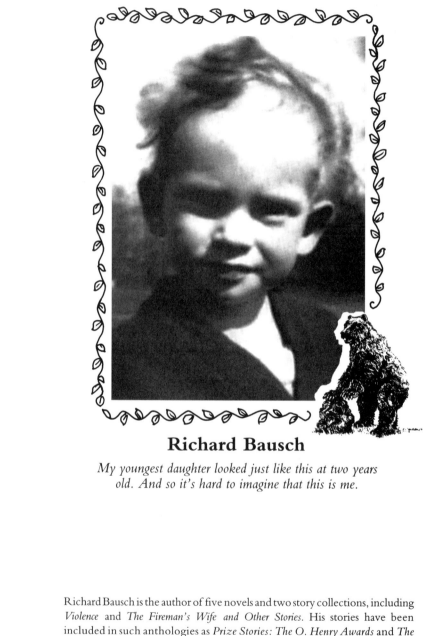

Richard Bausch

My youngest daughter looked just like this at two years old. And so it's hard to imagine that this is me.

Richard Bausch is the author of five novels and two story collections, including *Violence* and *The Fireman's Wife and Other Stories*. His stories have been included in such anthologies as *Prize Stories: The O. Henry Awards* and *The Best American Short Stories*, and have won the National Magazine Award in both 1988 and 1990. *Rebel Powers*, his sixth novel, was published in April 1993.

Bausch lives in Broad Run, Virginia.

RICHARD BAUSCH

Weather

Carla headed out to White Elks Mall in the late afternoon, accompanied by her mother, who hadn't been very glad of the necessity of going along, and said so. She went on to say what Carla already knew: that she would brave the August humidity and the discomfort of the hot car if it meant she wouldn't be in the house alone when Carla's husband came back from wherever he had gone that morning. "It's bad enough without me asking for more trouble by being underfoot," she said.

"Nobody thinks you're underfoot, Mother. You didn't have to come."

They were quiet after that. Carla had the Saturday traffic to contend with. Her mother stared out at the gathering thunderclouds above the roofs of the houses they passed. The wind was picking up; it would storm. Carla's mother was the sort of person who liked to sit and watch the scenery while someone else drove. It was a form of concentration with her, almost as solemn as prayer. Now and then she would comment on what she saw, and one could answer or not; it made little difference.

"I hope we get there before it starts to rain," she said now.

Carla was looking in her side-view mirror, slowing the car. "Go on, idiot. Go on by."

Glimmer Train Stories, Issue 11, Summer 1994

"We don't have an umbrella," Mother said.

Lightning cut through the dark mass of clouds to the east.

"I have to watch the road," Carla said, and then blew her horn at someone who had veered too close, changing lanes in front of them. "God, how I hate this town."

For a while there was just the sound of the rocker arms tapping in the engine, and the gusts of wind buffeting the sides of the car. The car was low on oil—another expense, another thing to worry about. It kept losing oil. You had to check it every week or so and it always registered a quart low. Something was leaking somewhere.

"Well, this storm might cool us all off."

"Not supposed to," Carla said, ignoring the other woman's tone. "They're calling for muggy heat."

When they pulled into White Elks, Mother said, "You know, I never liked all the stores in one building like this. I used to so love going into the city to do my shopping. Walking along the street looking in all the windows. And seeing people going about their business, too. There's something—I don't know—reassuring about a busy city street in the middle of the day. Of course we would never go when it was like this."

The rain came now—big, heavy drops.

"Where're we going, anyway?"

"I told you," Carla said. "Record World. I have to buy a tape for Beth's birthday." She parked the car and they hurried across to the closest entrance—the Sears appliance store. Inside, they shook the water from their hair and looked at each other.

"It's going to be all right, Honey."

"Mother, please. You keep saying that."

"Well?" Mother said. "It's true. Sometimes you have to say the truth, like a prayer or a chant. It needs saying, Honey. It makes a pressure to be spoken."

Carla shook her head.

"I won't utter another syllable," said Mother.

At the display-crowded doorway of the record store, a man wearing a blue blazer over a white T-shirt and jeans paused to let the two of them enter before him.

"Thank you," Mother said, smiling. "Such a considerate young man."

But then a clap of thunder startled them all, and they paused, watching the high-domed skylight above them flash with lightning. The tinted glass was streaked with water, and the wind swept the rain across the surface in sheets. It looked as though something was trying to break through the window and get at the dry, lighted, open space below. Other shoppers stopped and looked up. Everybody was wearing the bright colors and sparse clothing of summer—shorts and T-shirts, sleeveless blouses and

tank tops, even a bathing suit or two—and the severity of the storm made them seem oddly exposed, oddly vulnerable, as though they could not possibly have come from the outdoors, where the elements raged and the sunlight had died out of the sky. One very heavy woman in a red jumpsuit with a pattern of tiny white sea horses across the waistband said, "Looks like it's going to be a twister," to no one in particular, then strolled on by. This was not an area of Virginia that had ever been known to have a tornado.

"What would a twister do to a place like this, I wonder," Mother said.

"It's just a thunderstorm."

But the wind seemed to gather sudden force, and something banged at the roof in the vicinity of the window.

"Lord," Mother said. "It's violent, whatever it is."

They remained where they were, watching the skylight. Carla lighted a cigarette.

"Excuse me," the man in the blue blazer said. "Could you please let me pass."

She looked at him. Large, round eyes the color of water under beams of sun, dark black hair, and bad skin. A soft, downturning mouth. Perhaps thirty or so. There was unhappiness in the face; she had seen it.

"Can I pass, please," he said impatiently.

"You're in his way," Mother said. They both laughed, moving aside. "We got interested in the storm."

"Maybe you'd both like to have a seat and watch to your hearts' content," the man said. "After all, this only happens to be a doorway."

"All you have to do is say what you want," said Carla.

He went on into the store.

"And a good day to you, too."

"I swear," Mother said. "The rudeness of some people."

They moved to the bench across the way and sat down. The

bench was flanked by two fat white columns, each with a small metal ashtray attached to it. Carla smoked her cigarette and stared at the people walking by. Her mother fussed with the small strap of her purse, and then looked through the purse for a napkin, with which she gingerly wiped some rainwater from the side of her face. The water had smeared her makeup, and she attended to that. Above them, the storm went on, and briefly the lights flickered. A leak was coming from somewhere, and water ran in a thin, slow stream down the opposite wall. Carla smoked the cigarette automatically.

"You know, I've always had this perverse wish to actually see a tornado," said Mother.

"I saw one when Daryl and I lived in Illinois—just before Beth was born. No thank you." Carla took a last drag on the cigarette, placed it in the metal ashtray attached to the column, and clicked the mouth shut. Then she opened the mouth and clicked it shut again.

"You're brooding, aren't you?" Mother said.

"I'm not brooding," Carla said. She took another cigarette out of the pack in her purse and lighted it.

"Well, I didn't come with you to watch you smoke."

"We've established why you came with me, Mother."

"I don't see why I have to watch you smoke."

"I didn't ask you to watch me smoke. Leave me alone, will you?"

"I won't say another word."

"And don't get your feelings hurt, either."

"You're the boss. God knows it's none of my business. I'm only a spectator here."

"Oh, please."

They were quiet. Somewhere behind them, a baby fussed. "What were you thinking about?" Mother said. "You were thinking about this morning, right?"

"I was thinking about how unreal everything is."

"You don't mean the storm, though, do you."

"No, Mother—I don't mean the storm."

"Well, but we need the storm. The rain, I mean. I mean I'm glad it's storming."

"I'm not surprised, since a minute ago you were wishing it was a tornado."

"I was doing no such thing. I was merely expressing an element of my personality. A—a curiousness, that's all. And, anyway, that's not what I'm talking about. Let me finish. You never let me finish, Carla. You're always jumping the gun, and you've always done that. You did it to Daryl this morning—went right ahead and finished his sentences for him."

Carla shook her head. "I can't help it if I know what he's going to say before he says it."

They were quiet again. Mother stirred restlessly in her seat and watched the trickle of water run down the wall opposite where they sat. Finally, she leaned toward the younger woman and murmured, "I was going to say it's just weather. This morning, you know. You're both just going through a little spell of bad weather. Daryl's still got some growing up to do, God knows. But all of them do. I never met a man who couldn't use a little growing up. And Daryl's a perfect example of that."

"I think I've figured out how you feel about him, Mother."

"Well, no—I admit sometimes I think you'd be better off if he *did* move out. I promised I wouldn't interfere, though."

"You're not interfering," Carla said in the voice of someone who felt interfered with.

"I *will* say I don't like the way he talks to you."

"Oh, please—let's change the subject."

"Well, I for one am happy to change the subject. You think I'm enjoying talking about it? You think I enjoy seeing you and that boy say those things to each other?"

"Oh, for God's sake. He's not a boy, Mother. He's your son-in-law, and you're stuck with him." Carla blew smoke. "At least for the time being."

"Don't talk like that. And I was just using a figure of speech."

"It happens to make him very mad."

"Well, he's not here, right now."

She smoked the cigarette, watching the people walk by. A woman came past pushing a double stroller with twins in it.

"Look," said Mother. "How sweet."

"I see them." Carla had only glanced at them.

"You're so—hard-edged sometimes, Carla. You never used to be that way, no matter how unhappy things made you."

"What? I looked. What did you want me to do?"

"I swear, I just don't understand anything anymore."

After a pause, Mother said, "I remember when you were that small. Your father liked to put you on his chest and let you nap there. Seems like weeks—just a matter of days ago."

Carla took a long drag of the cigarette, blew smoke, and watched it. She had heard it said somewhere that blind persons do not generally like cigarettes as much as sighted people, for not being able to watch the smoke.

"But men were more respectful somehow, in our day."

"Look, please—"

"I'll shut up."

"I'm sure it'll be all made up before the day's over."

"Oh, I know—you'll give in, and he'll say he forgives you. Like every other time."

"We'll forgive each other."

"I'm not uttering another word," Mother said. "I know I cause tension by talking. It's no secret he hates me—"

"He doesn't hate you. You drive him crazy—"

"I drive him crazy? He sits in the living room with that guitar of his plunking around, even when the television is on—never finishing—have you ever heard him play a whole song all the way through? It would be one thing if he could play notes. But that constant strumming—"

"He's trying to learn. That's all. It's a project."

"Well, it drives me right up the wall."

A pair of skinny boys came running from one end of the open space, one chasing the other and trying to keep up. Behind them a woman hurried along, carrying a handful of small flags.

"Do I drive *you* crazy?" Mother wanted to know.

"All the time," Carla said. "Of course."

"I'm serious."

"Well, don't be. Let's not be serious, okay?"

"You're the one that's been off in another world all afternoon. I don't blame you, of course."

"Mother," Carla said.

"I'm not going to get into it. I'm not going to make another sound."

"Things are hard for him right now, that's all. He's not used to being home all day—"

"If you ask me, he could've had that job at the shoe store."

"He's not a shoe salesman. He's an engineer. He's trained for something. That was what they all said when we were growing up, wasn't it? Train for something? Wasn't that what they said? Plan for the future and get an education so you'd be ready? Well, what if the future isn't anything like what you planned for, Mother?"

"Well—but listen—it's like I said, Honey. You're both in a stormy period, and you just have to sit it out, that's all. But the day your father ever called me stupid—I'd have shown him the door, let me tell you. I'd have slapped his face."

"Daryl didn't call me stupid. He said that something I said was the stupidest thing he ever heard. And what I said *was* stupid."

"Oh, listen to you."

"It was. I said the money he was spending on gas driving back and forth to coach little league was going to cost Beth her college education."

"That's a valid point, if you ask me."

"Oh, come on. I was mad and I said anything. I just wanted to hit at him."

"Well, it's not the stupidest thing he ever heard. I'm certain that over the last month I've said three or four hundred things he thinks are more stupid."

Carla smiled.

"And he still shouldn't talk that way."

"We were having an argument, Mother."

"All right—just like I told you. A little storm. It shouldn't ruin your whole day."

Carla looked down, took the last drag of her cigarette.

"You just have to set the boundaries a little. I mean your father never—"

"I'm going into the record store, Mother."

"I know. I came with you, didn't I? You ought to get something for yourself. I hope you spend your own money on yourself for once. Get whatever Beth wants for her birthday and then get something for yourself."

"Beth wants a rap record, and I can't remember the name of it."

"Oh, God," said Mother. "I don't like that stuff. I don't even like people who *do* like it."

"Beth likes it."

"Beth's thirteen. What does she know?"

"She knows what she wants for her birthday." Carla sighed. "I know what I have to get and how much it's going to cost and how much I'll hate having it blaring in the house all day, too. I just don't remember the name of it."

"Maybe it'll come to you," said Mother.

"It'll have to."

"Of course, you could forget it, couldn't you?"

"It's the only thing she asked for."

"Well, what if the only thing she asked for was a trip to Rome, or—or a big truckload of drugs or something?"

Carla looked at her.

"Well?"

"The two go together so naturally, Mother. I always think of truckloads of drugs when I think of Rome."

"You know what I mean."

"Did you ever do that to me?" Carla asked. "Lie to me that way?"

"Of course not. I wouldn't dream of such a thing."

"How can you suggest that I do it to Beth?"

"It was an idea—it had to do with self-preservation. If she hadn't been playing her music so loud this morning, Daryl and you might not've got into it."

Carla looked at her.

"You have my solemn vow."

"Anyway," Carla said. "You can't put this morning off on Beth."

Mother made a gesture, like turning a key in a lock, at her lips.

"The fact is, we don't need any excuses to have a fight, these days."

"Now don't get down on yourself, Honey. You've had enough to deal with. I should never have moved in. I try to mind my own business—"

"You're fine. This has nothing to do with you. It was going on before you moved in. It's been going on a long time."

"Honey, it's nothing you can't solve. The two of you."

"Unreal," Carla said, bringing a handkerchief out of her purse. "It seems everything I do makes him mad."

"We're all getting on each other's nerves," said Mother.

"Let me just have a minute, here." Carla turned slightly, facing the column, wiping her eyes with the handkerchief.

"Don't you worry, Sweetie."

"We just have to get on the other side of it," Carla said.

"That's right. Daryl just has to settle down and see how lucky he is. I won't say anything else about it. It's not my place to say anything."

"Mother, will you please stop that? You can say anything you want. I give you my permission."

"I don't have another thing to add."

"Let's just do what we came to do," Carla said. "I don't want to think about anything else right now."

"No, and you shouldn't have to, and you live in a house where you have to think of absolutely everything."

"That isn't true. It's not just Daryl, Mother."

"All right," Mother said. "I'm sorry. I should keep my mouth shut."

Carla hesitated, looked around herself. She ran one hand through her hair, and sighed again. "Sometimes I—I think—we were going to have a big family—we both wanted a lot of children, you know, and maybe it's because I couldn't—God, never mind."

"Oh, no—now that's not it at all. You're imagining that. He's been out of work and that always makes tension. I mean, Daryl's got a lot of things wrong with him, but he'd never blame you for something you can't help."

"But you read about tension over one thing making other tensions worse."

"That doesn't have anything to do with you," Mother said.

"When we had Beth it—nothing about that pregnancy—you know, it was full term. Everything went so well."

"Carla, you don't really think he'd hold anything against you."

"I hope not. But Mother, he was so crestfallen the last time."

"Well, and so were you."

"The thing is, we always pulled together before—when there was any trouble at all. We'd cling to each other. You remember when he was just out of college and there wasn't any work and he was doing all those part-time jobs—we were so happy then. Beth was small. We didn't have anything and we didn't want anything, really."

"Well, you're older now. And you've got your mother living with you."

"No, that's what you don't understand. I told you—this was going on before you moved in. That's the truth. In fact, it got better for a little while, those first days after you moved in. It was like—it seemed that having you with us brought something of the old times back, you know?"

"Don't divide it up like that, Honey. It's still your time together. There's no old times or new times. That isn't how you should think about it. It's the two of you. And this is weather. Weather comes and changes and you keep on. That's all."

Carla put the handkerchief back in her purse. "Do I look like I've been crying?"

"You look like the wrath of God."

They laughed nervously, not quite returning each other's gaze. The crowd was moving around them, and though the thunder and lightning had mostly ceased, the rain still beat against the skylight.

"Really, Honey," Mother said. "Your father and I had these bad spells, too."

"Well," said Carla, "on with the show."

"That's the spirit."

They walked into the store. The man in the blue blazer was standing by a rack of compact discs that were being sold at a clearance price. He'd already chosen several, and had them tucked under his arm. He was rifling through the discs, apparently looking for something specific, that he would recognize on sight; he wasn't pausing long enough to read the titles. Concentrating, he looked almost angry; the skin around his eyes was white. He glanced at the two women as they edged past him, and Mother said, "Excuse us," rather pointedly. He did not answer, but went back to thumbing through the discs.

The store was very crowded, and there wasn't much room to

move around. Carla and her mother made their way along the aisle to the audiotape section, where Carla recognized the tape she had come for. It was in a big display on the wall, with a life-size poster of the artist.

"Looks like a mugger, if you ask me," Mother said. She picked up something for herself—an anthology of songs from the sixties. "The Beatles actually wore ties at one point, you know." Somewhere speakers were pounding with percussion, the drone of a toneless, shrill male voice.

"I think that's what I'm about to buy," said Carla. "God help me."

There were two lines waiting at the counter, and the two women stood side by side, each in her own line. The man in the blazer stepped in behind Mother. He had several discs in his hands, and he began reading one of the labels. Carla glanced at him, so dour, and she thought of Daryl, off somewhere angry with her, unhappy—standing under the gaze of someone else, who would see it in his face. When the man looked up, she sent a smile in his direction, but he was staring at the two girls behind the counter, both of whom were dressed in the bizarre getup of rock stars. The girls chattered back and forth, being witty and funny with each other in that attitude store clerks sometimes have when people are lined up waiting: as though circumstances had provided them with an audience, and as though the audience were entertained by their talk. The clerks took a long time with each purchase, running a scanner over the coded patch on the tapes and discs, and then punching numbers into the computer terminals. The percussion thrummed in the walls, and the lines moved slowly. When Mother's turn came, she reached for Carla. "Here, Honey—step in here."

Carla did so.

"Wait a minute," the man said. "You can't do that."

"Do what?" Mother said. "She's waiting with me."

"She was in the other line."

"We were waiting together."

"You were in separate lines." The man addressed the taller of the two girls behind the counter. "They were in separate lines."

"I don't know," the girl said. Her hair was an unnatural shade of orange. She held her hands up as if in surrender, and bracelets clattered on her wrist. Then she moved to take Carla's tape and run the scanner over it.

"Oh, well—all right," the man said. "Let stupidity and selfishness win out."

Mother faced him. "What did you say? Did you call my daughter a name?"

"You heard everything I said," the man told her.

"Yes, I did," Mother said, and swung at his face. He backpedaled, but took the blow above the eye, so that he almost lost his balance. When he had righted himself, he stood straight, wide-eyed, clearly unable to believe what had just happened to him.

"Lady," the man said. "You—"

And Mother struck again, this time swinging her purse so that it hit the man on the crown of the head as he ducked, putting his arms up to ward off the next blow. His discs fell to the floor at his feet.

"Mother—" Carla began, not quite hearing herself. "What in the world—"

"You don't call my daughter names and get away with it," Mother said to the man.

He had straightened again, and assumed the stance of someone in a fight, his fists up to protect his face, chin tucked into his left shoulder.

"You think you can threaten me," Mother said, and poked at his face with her free hand. He blocked this, and stepped back, and she swung the purse again, striking him this time on the forearm.

"Oh, God—please," said Carla, barely breathing the words.

There was a general commotion in the crowd. Someone laughed.

"This isn't right," Carla said. "Let's stop this—"

"Well, look at him. Big tough man—going to hit a woman, big tough guy?"

"I want the police," the man said to the girl with the orange hair. "I absolutely demand to see a policeman. I've been assaulted and I intend to press charges."

"Oh, look," Carla said, "can you just forget about it? Here." She bent down to pick up the discs he had dropped.

"Don't you dare," Mother said.

Carla looked at her.

"All right, I'll shut up. But don't you dare give him those discs."

Carla ignored her.

"I want to see a policeman."

"Here," Carla said, offering the discs.

"If he says another thing—"

The man looked past them. "Officer, I've been assaulted. And there are all these witnesses."

A security guard stepped out of the crowd. He was thin, green-eyed, blond, with boyish skin. Perhaps he had to shave once a week. But clearly he took great care with all aspects of his appearance: his light-blue uniform was creased exactly, the shirt starched and pressed. His shoes shone like twin black mirrors. He brought a writing pad out of his pocket, and a ballpoint pen, the end of which he clicked with his thumb. "Okay, what happened here?"

"He called my daughter a name," said Mother. "I won't have people calling my daughter names."

"I'm pressing charges," said the man.

The security guard addressed him. "Would you just say what happened?"

But everyone began to speak at once. The girl with the orange hair put her hands up again in surrender, and again the bracelets clattered. "None of my business," she said. "I don't believe in violence." She spoke in an almost metaphysical tone, the tone of someone denying a belief in the existence of a thing like violence. Carla was trying to get the officer's attention, and then he was drawing her mother and the man out of the store, into the open area of shops, under the skylight. She followed. Mother and the man protested all the way, accusing each other.

"I've got a welt," the man said. "Right here." He pointed to his left eyebrow.

"I don't see it," said the officer.

"Do you have jurisdiction here?"

"I have that, yes. I have the authority."

"I've been attacked. And I want to file a complaint."

"This man verbally assaulted my daughter."

"All right, all right," said the security guard. "Calm down. We're not going to get anywhere like this. I'll listen to you one at a time."

"This man verbally assaulted my daughter. And I slapped him."

"You didn't slap me. You hit me with your fist, and then you assaulted me with your purse."

"I didn't hit you with my fist. If I'd hit you with my fist, that would be an assault."

"Both of you be quiet for a minute." He stood there writing in the pad. "Let me have your names."

Both Mother and the man spoke at once.

"Wait a minute," the officer said. "For God's sake. One at a time."

"Please," said Carla. "Couldn't we just forget this?"

"I don't want to forget it," said the man. "I was attacked. A person ought to be able to walk into a store without being attacked."

"My sentiments exactly," said Mother. "You started it. You

attacked my daughter verbally."

"Both of you be quiet or I'm going to cite you," the security guard said.

They stood there.

"What's your name, sir?"

"Todd Lemke."

The officer wrote it down on his pad. "Like it sounds?"

"One *e*."

"All right. You start."

"I was waiting in line, and this woman—" Lemke indicated Carla.

"You be careful how you say that," said Mother.

"Now, ma'am—" the security guard said.

"I won't let people talk about my daughter that way, young man. And I don't care what you or anybody else says about it." Her voice had reached a pitch Carla had never heard before.

"Please, ma'am."

"I won't say another word. But he better watch his tone. That's all I have to say."

"Mother, if you don't shut up," Carla said. There were tears in her voice.

"What did I say? I just indicated that I wouldn't tolerate abuse. This man abused you, didn't you hear it?"

"Ma'am, I'm afraid I'm going to have to insist."

"Pitiful," Lemke was saying, shaking his head. "Just pitiful."

"Who's pitiful?" Carla said. She moved toward him. She could feel her heart beating in her face and neck. "Who's pitiful?"

The security guard stood between them. "Now look—"

"You watch who you call names," Carla said, and something slipped inside her. The next moment anything might happen.

"I rest my case," Lemke was saying.

"There isn't any case," Carla said. "You don't have any case. Nobody's pitiful."

"They're making my case for me, officer."

"—such disrespect—" Mother was saying.

"You're wrong about everything," Carla said. "Pity doesn't enter into it."

"Everybody shut up," the security guard said. "I swear I'm going to run you all in for disturbing the peace."

"Do I have to say anything else?" Lemke said to him. "It's like I said. They make my case for me—ignorant—lowlife—"

"I'm going to hit him again," said Mother. "You're the one who's ignorant."

"See? She admits she hit me."

"I'm going to hit you myself in a minute," the security guard said. "Now shut up."

The man gave him an astonished look.

"Everybody be quiet." He held his hands out and made a slow, up-and-down motion with each word, like a conductor in front of an orchestra. "Let's—all—of—us—just—calm—down." He turned to Mother. "You and your daughter please wait here. I'll come back to you."

"Yes, sir."

"We'll be here," Carla said.

"Now," he said to Lemke, "if you'll just step over here with me, I'll listen to what you have to say."

"You're biased against me," Lemke said.

"I'm what?"

"You heard me. You threatened to hit me."

"For God's sake."

"No. I'm not going to get a fair deal here, I can sense it."

"We're not in a courtroom, sir. This is not a courtroom."

"I know what kind of report you'll file."

"Look, I'm sure if we all give each other the benefit of the doubt a little—"

"This woman assaulted me," Lemke said. "I know my rights."

"Okay," the security guard said. "Why don't you tell me what you want me to do. I mean really—what it is that you think I should do here?"

Lemke stared into his face.

"I think he wants you to shoot me," Mother said.

"Mother, will you please stop it. Please."

"Her own daughter can't control her," Lemke said. "You shouldn't take her out of the house."

"I'm pregnant," Carla said abruptly, and began to cry. The tears came streaming down her cheeks. It was a lie; she had said it simply to cut through everything.

Her mother had taken a step back. "Oh, Honey—"

And Carla went on talking, only now she was telling the truth: "I've lost the last four. Do you understand, sir? I've miscarried four times and I need someone with me. Surely, even you can understand that."

Lemke stared at her, and something changed in his face. His whole body seemed to falter slightly, as though he had been supporting some invisible weight, and had now let down under it. But only a little. "Look, hey—" he stammered. "Listen—"

"Why don't you all make friends," said the security guard. "No harm done, really. Right?"

"Right," Mother said. "My daughter had a little—a tiff with her husband this morning, and he said some things. Maybe I overreacted. I overreacted. I'm really sorry, sir."

Lemke was staring at Carla.

"I don't know my own strength sometimes," Mother was saying. "I'm always putting my foot in it."

"A misunderstanding," the security guard said.

Lemke rubbed the side of his face, looking at Carla, who was wiping her eyes with the back of one hand.

"Am I needed here anymore?" the security guard said.

"No," said Lemke, "I guess not."

"There," said Mother. "Now, could anything have worked out better?"

"I have to tell you," Lemke said to Carla, and it seemed to her that his voice shook. "We lost our first last month. My wife was seven months pregnant. She's had a hard time of it since."

"We're sorry that happened to you," Mother said.

"Mother," said Carla, sniffling. "Please."

"I hope things work out for you," Lemke said to her.

"Do you have other children?" Carla asked.

He nodded. "A girl."

"Us, too."

"How old?"

"Thirteen."

"Seven," Lemke said. "Pretty age."

"Yes."

"They're all lovely ages," Mother said.

"Thank you for understanding," Carla said to him.

"No," he said. "It's—I'm sorry for everything." Then he moved off. In a few seconds, he was lost in the crowd.

"I guess he didn't want his discs, after all," Mother said. Then: "Poor man. Isn't it amazing that you'd find out in an argument that you have something like that in common—"

"What're the chances," Carla said, almost to herself. Then she turned to Mother. "Do you think I could've sensed it somehow, or heard it in his voice?"

Mother smiled out of one side of her mouth. "I think it's a coincidence."

"I don't know," Carla said. "I feel like I knew."

"That's how I think I felt about you being pregnant. I just had this feeling."

"I'm not pregnant," Carla told her.

Mother frowned, staring.

"I couldn't stand the arguing anymore, and I just said it."

"Oh, my."

"Poor Daryl," Carla said, after a pause. "Up against me all by himself."

"Stop that," said Mother.

"Up against us."

"I won't listen to you being contrite."

Carla started back into the store, and when her mother started to follow her, she stopped. "I'll buy yours for you," she said. "Let me get in line."

"You know, I can't believe I actually hit that boy." Mother held out one hand, palm down, gazing at it. "Look at me—I'm shaking all over. I'm trembling all over. I've never done anything like that in my life, not ever. Not even close. I mean, I've never even yelled at anyone in public, have I? I mean, think of it. *Me*, in a public brawl. My God. This morning must've set me up or something. I mean, set the tone, you know. Got me primed. I'd never have expected this of me, would you?"

"I don't think anyone expected it," Carla said.

They watched the woman with the twin babies come back by them.

"And I feel sorry for him, now," Mother said. "I almost wish I hadn't hit him. I mean, if I'd known, you know—I could've tried to give him the benefit of the doubt, like the officer said."

Carla said nothing. She had stopped crying. Her mascara was running down her cheeks. Her mother took out a handkerchief, wet it with her tongue, and touched the smeared places.

"Everybody has their own troubles, I guess."

Carla went to the counter, where people moved back to let her buy the tapes. It took only a moment.

Mother stood in the entrance of the store, looking pale and frightened.

"Come on, Sugar Ray," Carla said to her.

"You're mad at me," Mother said, and seemed about to cry herself.

"I'm not mad," Carla said.

"I'm so sorry—I can't imagine what got into me—can't imagine. But, Honey, I hear him talk to you that way. It hurts to hear him say those things to you and I know I shouldn't interfere—"

"It's all right," Carla told her. "Really. I understand."

Outside, they waited in the lee of the building for the rain to let up. The air had grown much cooler; there was a breeze blowing out of the north. The treeline on the other side of the parking lot moved, and showed lighter green.

"My God," Carla said. "Isn't it—doesn't it say something about me that I would use the one gravest sadness in Daryl's life with me—the one thing he's always been most sorry about—that I would use that to get through an altercation at the fucking mall?"

"Stop it," Mother said.

"Well, really. And I didn't even have to think about it. I was crying, and I saw the look on his face, and I just said it. It came out so naturally. And imagine—me lying that I'm pregnant again. Imagine Daryl's reaction to that."

"You're human—what do you want from yourself?"

Carla seemed not to have heard this. "I wish I *was* pregnant," she said. "I feel awful, and I really wish I was."

"That wouldn't change anything, would it?"

"It would change how I feel right now."

"I meant with Daryl."

Carla looked at her. "No. You're right," she said. "That wouldn't change anything with Daryl. Not these days."

"Now, Honey," Mother said, touching her nose with the handkerchief.

But then Carla stepped out of the protection of the building and was walking away through the rain.

"Hey," Mother said. "Wait for me."

The younger woman turned. "I'm going to bring the car up. Stay there."

"Well, let a person know what you're going to do, for God's sake."

"Wait there," Carla said over her shoulder.

The rain was lessening now. She got into the car and sat thinking about her mother in the moment of striking the man

with her purse. She saw the man's startled face in her mind's eye and, to her surprise, she laughed, once, harshly, like a sob. Then she was crying again, thinking of her husband, who would not come home today until he had to. Across the lot, her mother waited, a blur of colors, a shape in the raining distance. Mother put the handkerchief to her face again, and then seemed to falter. Carla started the car and backed out of the space, aware that the other woman could see her now, and trying to master herself, wanting to put the best face on, wanting not to hurt any more feelings and to find some way for everyone to get along, to bear the disappointments and the irritations; and as she pulled toward the small, waiting figure under the wide stone canopy, she caught herself thinking, with a wave of exhaustion, as though it were a prospect she would never have enough energy or strength for, no matter how hard or long she strove to gain it, of what was constantly required—what must be repeated and done and given and listened to and allowed—in all the kinds of love there are.

Her mother stepped to the curb and opened the door. "What were you doing?" she said, struggling into the front seat. "I thought you were getting ready to leave me here."

"No," Carla said, "Never that." Her voice went away.

Her mother shuffled a lot on the seat, getting settled, then pulled the door shut. The rain was picking up again, though it wasn't wind-driven now.

"Can't say I'd blame you if you left me behind," Mother said. "After all, I'm clearly a thug."

They were silent for a time, sitting there in the idling car with the rain pouring down. And then they began to laugh. It was low, almost tentative, as if they were both uneasy about letting go entirely. The traffic paused and moved by them, and shoppers hurried past.

"I really can't believe I did such an awful thing," Mother said.

"I won't listen to you being contrite," Carla said, and smiled.

"All right, Sweetie. You scored your point."

"I wasn't trying to score points," Carla told her. "I was setting the boundaries for today." Then she put the car in gear and headed them through the rain, toward home.

Pluggers

Pluggers have ways to deal with writer's block.

Robert Bausch

My mother and father had six children and here we all are. My older sister, Barbara (holding the baby), had four babies of her own. She was a lovely young woman who also dreamed of being a writer. In 1974, when she was just thirty-two, she and her husband were killed in an automobile accident. My parents raised her children. Richard, my twin brother and also a writer (five novels, two story collections), is on the far left. Steve, who now manages a clothing store, is next to him. Timmy, the baby in Barbara's arms, owns a lighting distributorship. My sister Betty has four children and a happy family of her own and she is one of the few people on earth whose respect I would hate to lose. I am on the right. The photo was taken by the Washington Post *because my sister Barbara had just written an essay nominating my father for "Father of the Year." It was a great family to grow up with.*

Robert Bausch has published three novels: *On the Way Home*, *The Lives of Riley Chance*, and *Almighty Me!* He is nearly finished with a fourth novel, which he is now calling *A Hole in the Earth*, and has also just recently completed a collection of short stories that he is calling *Animal Stories*. *Almighty Me!* was sold to Hollywood Films, a division of Disney studios, and may someday be a feature film.

ROBERT BAUSCH

Family Lore

In the car, on the way to visit his father, Dad tells me once again the story of the encore fish. I have heard it many times, but today I am courteous and attentive. I have come to see my father this summer because he is alone now, and everyone keeps telling me he misses me. I live on the West Coast with Gordon, my second husband, who is new to families and saw no reason to make this trip. He has talked to my father once or twice on the phone, but we have not been married long enough for him to feel any obligation where my father is concerned. I have been told to say hello.

Although we live just across the bay from San Francisco, near enough to the water to see Alcatraz, I tell my friends I am glad to live as far as I can get from Baltimore and its harbor songs and uniform marble steps. I am here in Baltimore now because this is where my father lives and, if I want to see him, I know I have to come here.

The story of the encore fish is as funny as any I've heard my father tell, and since we are trapped in traffic, the air conditioner blowing weakly cooled air in my face, the car inching forward every few minutes, it seems a good way to pass the time.

My father likes the story because he's the hero in it, and

Glimmer Train Stories, Issue 11, Summer 1994

because it is about one of the few times he was given the pleasure of putting one over on his brother Phil.

Uncle Phil, the oldest of my grandfather's children, has never failed at anything. My father calls him "Phil the Pill." He was the one who braved far-away colleges, testy scholarship committees, and difficult curricula. He has four degrees: a B.S. in math, a B.A. in English, an M.A. in philosophy, and a law degree from Loyola of Chicago. He has actually sky-dived. He's hiked the Appalachian Trail and ridden a small burro down a ribbon of ledge along the Grand Canyon. In spite of his intellect and education, every now and then he demonstrates his unreasoning faith in God by saying, "God love ya." He thinks women should bring in the snacks.

My father's other brother, the middle son, Robert, is the "hard-working high achiever" in the family—I'm quoting my grandfather. Robert is the self-made success story you read about in the Sunday *Parade* magazine. Unlike my father, Uncle Robert worked his way through college and is now a stockbroker and investment counselor who "pulls down" $200,000 a year. Robert owns a boat and spends every weekend on it, even in late fall when the weather turns really cold. I once heard him say he hates Christmas because he has to take his boat out of the water in December and he can't put it back until late March. During the Christmas season, he's mean and spiteful. It's as though the real Uncle Robert emerges. When you lift a boat out of the water, the underside of it is soiled and overlaid with green slime. This reminds me of my uncle Robert.

I have a brother and a sister. These are the people who have been telling me that my father needs to see me, that he is alone and cannot be left alone. My sister, Annette, married a heart doctor and lives in Cincinnati. She visits Father several times a year. She's always here at Christmas and sometimes Thanksgiving. She calls me once or twice a month and we have long conversations about her children. She also sometimes mentions

Dad. She tells me he really does miss me.

"He loves you because you're the youngest, just like he was," she says. I always hear her children clattering in the background.

I tell her it is a long trip and I can't afford to make it very often. She understands. Of all the talents Annette possesses, understanding is the most highly developed. I am not being ironic. She is the most thoughtful and tolerant person I've ever known. She was the first one in my family to welcome me back again after my divorce. My brother, Richard, would not speak to me until I'd remarried.

Of course I understood my brother's ire. I divorced his best friend. I couldn't help it. Richard's friend was the world's most underdeveloped biped personality. When I married James, I was only seventeen. I thought he was cute. He was strong, tan, twenty-one, and I was the last child at home. I wanted very much to begin my perfect life. I did not know James very well, but gradually I learned to dislike him. He wept when the Baltimore Colts moved to Indianapolis. When I had my first miscarriage, he was so moved he missed an episode of "M★A★S★H". (Later, I found out he had taped it so he could watch it when he was feeling better.) The next morning he made coffee.

My father was pretty upset about the divorce, too, but that was years ago and now we are riding in the car, just he and I, and he tells me the story of the encore fish.

"I always felt a little bit like the devil in Phil's presence," he says, warming up to it. "Once, when I was still in high school, he took me fishing at a lake up in Pennsylvania. He owned a cabin right on the water and he'd spend a week there with his family every year, but since I was becoming a young man, he wanted to get to know me better and become friends, as he put it. He thought it might be nice if the two of us went up there alone one year. We went in the fall, during the World Series. That year, the Cincinnati Reds were playing the Orioles. You know your uncle Phil. He's always been a Baltimore fan."

I smile and say, "We all are," although I don't care anymore about games of any kind.

"Anyway," Dad goes on, "the lake was so far out in the country we couldn't get the games on Phil's portable radio, but he had a powerful receiver and two-way radio in the cabin, which was only about twenty-five yards or so from the dock where we fished. He'd just get up every now and then and walk back to the cabin to check the score. We'd been fishing for most of the morning and he'd caught a fairly good-sized bass earlier that day. He took it off the hook and handed it to me. I didn't know what I was supposed to do with it. Phil says, 'The man who catches them hands them over to the man who didn't.' I just smiled at him. My mind was already working."

My father regularly smiles here, and just slightly winks an eye. It is a look of mischief laden with charm, and once again it makes me laugh. This encourages him.

"Phil says, 'Put it in the cooler.' He said it kindly, but it was still an order. Then he said, 'It's your turn, partner.' All morning he'd lectured me about manhood, and responsibility, and duty, and God's will in the world. He didn't ask me one question about anything in my life. He thought I needed saving. He thought everybody needed saving. I don't think he liked human beings very much, even then. He was always talking about changing the country, about bringing decency back to America. I remember having this vague feeling that I would not like it very much if people like Phil ran this country. He made me feel as though it was a sin to disagree with him."

"People like Phil do run this country," I say.

The traffic begins to pick up a bit, and he stops talking for a moment. At first, I think I should say something more, but he turns to me and smiles again. "You've heard this story a million times," he says.

"No, go ahead. I want to hear it again." I am telling the truth.

He looks ahead and says nothing.

"Really, Dad," I tell him. "I love this story. It's funny."

"Well," he says. "So we're fishing out on that pier and I'm pretty happy. Fishing is one of those joys that permits silence and solitude."

I say, "It's definitely not a boisterous activity."

He nods, barely pausing. "We're sitting there quietly and then Phil starts talking about God. 'Look across that lake,' he says. 'You see the design in the trees and the green underbrush and the clouds in the blue sky?' I tell him it's pretty, or something like that, and he says, 'You see how color-coordinated it all is? That's design.' I wanted to say what a great decorator God is, but I didn't want to offend him. To tell the truth, I really did feel as though I was sitting with Jesus."

I laugh out loud at this last. It is a new wrinkle, and it makes me happy to be truly amused again by the story. My father is equally pleased, his eyes shining now. Because he is driving, he cannot look at me, but I notice once more how fine his eyes are—the way they are bathed in clear liquid. The lines at the edge of his eyes seem to point to the light in each cornea. My mother told me many times that she fell in love with my father's eyes.

"I knew there was no way Phil and I would ever be friends," he says. "But he was determined to have a serious conversation with me, and when I realized that, I felt sorry for him. I wanted to try and make him laugh. I can only think of one other better thing to do to a human being besides make him laugh. The only trouble was, Phil never thought I was very funny." This also is painfully true. Whenever he gets together with his father and his brothers, they do all the talking. My father laughs with them and seems to enjoy himself, but he does not tell stories the way they do. They dramatize, and act out everything, even going so far as to imitate dialects and voices. Dad once said to me that he'd gone all his life trying to get a word in edgewise.

"Phil just thought I was a wise guy," Dad is saying. "But I really did want to make him laugh. So he concentrated on his line and didn't say anything for a while and I fell silent, too. A little later, he went to check on the ball score and I took the bass he had caught out of the cooler and put it on the end of his line and threw it back out into the water. Then I hollered, 'You got another one.'"

Here my father is beginning to laugh as he talks. He is enjoying this story as if it is the first time he has told it. The cars around us gleam in the hot sun and the air conditioner isn't working very well, but we are somehow transported to cooler places by my father's description of the lake and the breezes and Phil's encore fish.

"Phil comes running out. His line was moving in the water, the rod jittery and alive. He got this grin on his face and said, 'Damn, this is a good-sized one, too.' He reeled it in, took it off the hook. I offered to put it away, and took it from him. He sat there for a while, then he says, 'You're next.' I said, 'I'm not having any luck.' And he says, 'It ain't luck, hoss.' We fished silently for a while and then he went to check on the game again, and I took that same bass out of the cooler and put it on the end of his line."

My father is laughing as he speaks, and this infects me, too. I am laughing at first just because he is, but then in the middle of it, I realize it is real laughter and it makes me love him with the kind of tenderness I haven't felt in a long time. But I also feel sorry for him. He is delighted by this memory from his youth, by this triumph in his life. He is the only one of my grandfather's children who did not go to college. He has worked for almost thirty years at the post office. He has not had a bad life, but he does not think of his job as his life's work. He was happy, living with my mother and his three children, and now the children are gone, and three years ago, at the age of fifty-six, my mother choked to death on her own blood. She had just stopped smoking a few months before her lungs frothed up with red foam and she fell to the kitchen floor. My father wore a tie at her funeral—he looked at me, tears in his eyes and said, "I can't believe it, Honey. It's so hard to believe."

Now, he is laughing again. He is himself, and this makes me unreasonably happy. Hearing my father laugh produces a kind of drunkenness. "The second time," he says, "I let the fish down into the water gently and waited until Phil came back and picked up the rod. 'Holy smokes, I got another one,' he says. He was really excited. He fought with it a while and finally reeled it in. You should have seen his face. He goes, 'Man, that feels good.' He took it off the hook again and handed it to me and I placed it in the cooler. I don't know how I kept a straight face. I said, 'Well, you got me three to nothing.' And he says, 'You'll get one. You got to have patience.' He was so proud of himself, and you could see he was thinking of all those fish he was going to crowd into that cooler."

Dad stops for a moment, catching his breath. There is a long silence while the traffic begins to move at a normal pace and the air from the vents gets a bit cooler.

"The air conditioner works a lot better when we're moving," he says.

"I can't stand this heat."

"July's a pretty bad month around here, that's for sure."

"It's almost never this bad in 'Frisco."

It is quiet again, and I am beginning to think he wants to see if I will ask him to finish the story, so I do.

He smiles. "Where was I?"

"Phil's just caught his first fish for the third time."

He laughs. "Yeah."

He thinks for a minute, but this is just for effect. He knows where he is in the story. "Let's see, not much time went by before he went back to check the score again. I put the fish back on his line and threw it out into the water. He hollered from the cabin, 'Have I got another one?' and I said, 'I think so.' This time, he offered to give the line to me so I'd get the feel of it. He really was trying to be nice to me, and I have to remind myself all the time that he invited me to come with him to that lake so we could get to know one another."

He stops talking a moment, still smiling. The traffic has thinned out, and he puts both hands on the wheel and guns the car a bit. He's watching the road with a look of satisfaction. "I told Phil I'd catch one pretty soon. So he took the fish off his line and handed it to me. 'Four to nothing,' he said. He was so proud of his fishing skill. Soon, he started offering me tips. 'Let your line out a little; don't hold it so taut. The bait will move by itself in the currents.' We were at a lake, for Christ's sake! Lakes don't have currents. The water was absolutely still. If there were currents in there, they moved about as fast as a stopped clock."

He pauses, laughing now. I catch him glancing at me, to see if I'm laughing, too. "Your uncle Phil has always believed that if you just say a thing is true, it will be."

I have no response to this.

"That's why he's been such a successful lawyer."

I nod, agreeing—although I don't know what kind of lawyer my uncle is.

"Anyway," Father says, "after a while I asked Phil what the score of the game was. He says, 'It was nothing-nothing the last time I checked.' Then he tried to get me to go check the score, but I told him I hadn't caught anything yet and I was going to wait until I did. He set his rod down, got up, and said he'd go see if anything's happened. When he was inside the cabin, I took the fish out of the cooler and put it back on his line again. I swear the fish had an indignant look on its face."

We both enjoy the idea of the fish losing patience.

"A little later, Phil came back out and picked up his rod. He didn't notice anything on the line. 'Still nothing to nothing. They're in the seventh inning.' I didn't say anything. I'm watching his line. After ten minutes or so he says, 'You know what? I think I got another fish.' You should have seen him. He reeled it toward him, studied the end of his rod. The tip of it moved a tiny bit, the slightest little twitch. 'I do,' he says. 'I got another one.' He's reeling his line in and I'm pretending to be envious. 'Damn,' I said. 'Now you got me five to nothing.' And do you know what he says?"

The story always ends this way, and I know I have to answer. I wait just the right amount of time, looking at Dad, his smiling, expectant eyes, then I say, "What did he say?"

" 'This one's a little sluggish.' "

I laugh with him briefly and then I hear myself saying, "That's funny." I have always hated people who, when they hear a story, say things like that. It's an announcement that a person really doesn't appreciate humor. If a story is funny, then you laugh at it, you don't comment on how funny it is. My father knows this too—I think he taught it to me—so I am disconcerted to see that my remark has registered.

" 'This one's a little sluggish,' " he says again, his laughter sinking.

I am smiling at him, but I can't laugh. What I miss is the sound of my mother's laughter at times like this; "The Encore Fish" was her name for the story. I miss her now.

"Well," Dad says, "you've heard the story a thousand times."

"It really is funny," I say.

We ride in silence for a while. Although I know all these neighborhoods, these buildings, I really cannot recall how much farther it is to my grandfather's house. I am also fighting the sudden sensation that I do not want to go there. Not ever.

I don't understand why my father wants to make this visit. He seems as nervous about it as I am. He has confessed to me that he has not seen his father in a very long time, and I am beginning to believe that my visit to see my own father may have engendered this one to see his.

Watching the white steps pass by, I think of Gordon, my husband. I want to be free to do as I please and to have "my own problems," as he put it, but a part of me is still truly dismayed that he did not want to come here with me. He thinks I need this time with my father. That's what he said. He does not know me or my father, but I believe he was right, even though I know it was an excuse to stay in San Francisco.

My father sighs and says, "Dad will be glad to see you."

"How old is he now?"

"Seventy-seven."

I nod.

He looks at me briefly and then back to the road. "It's a short trip through here."

"I know," I say.

"Before you know it, you're fifty—and then ..." He breaks off and I know he is thinking of Mother.

I don't want to talk about it again, the way she died. He hates her for it, but he will never admit it. He blames doctors, the cigarettes. Sometimes he'll say, "She didn't have to keep smoking so much." It is as close as he gets to expressing his anger.

Just before we pull onto the street where my grandfather lives, I reach over and touch his arm. "I'm glad I came, Dad."

"Me, too," he says, tears in his eyes. "Me, too."

I am disturbed to discover that my uncle Phil is also visiting my grandfather. He seems surprised to see us, greets us at the door with a drink in his hand. "Come on in," he says, as though it is his house and family we have come all this way to visit. He has graying hair above his ears, a long, much more pointed nose than my father's. I hate the way he rattles the ice in his glass.

Dad says, "Hey, Phil."

"Little Shaver," Phil says. "It's good to see you."

My father looks at his shoes.

I step up and say, "He's a bit grown up to be called Little Shaver, don't you think?"

"It's a family nickname," Phil says, annoyed. We have argued over this before—at Mother's funeral. My father was weeping into his handkerchief, and I was standing across the way on the other side of the bier, trying not to cry, and I heard Phil say to Robert, "Poor Little Shaver. He really loved that woman."

I walked over and looked Phil in the eyes and whispered, "My father is a grown man. He raised a family, and now he's a widower."

Phil moved closer and leaned over. "Yes?" He gestured for me to finish the thought.

Like a fool, I started crying. He moved to put his arms around me, but I put my hand on his chest and stopped him. I said, "Don't call him Little Shaver, goddammit."

He stepped back, frowning. I thought he was going to rebuke me, but then what I said seemed to register. He stammered a bit, "Well, I'm—I'm—I'm sure I—" Then he said, "I'm sorry. I really am. I didn't know it bothered you."

"It bothers him," I said.

He nodded, and I turned, still sobbing, and roamed back to where I had been standing before. I could see my father, his face buried in his hands, his shoulders quavering, and I prayed for the last time in my life. I wanted him to lift his head and get control of himself.

My grandfather is glad to see me. He thinks I am Mother. "No, Dad," my father says. "This is my daughter, Nicole."

"Nicky," he says. His voice is strong. "Come over here and let me look at you."

I stand in front of him, feeling like a little girl.

"Well, you'd look much better in a dress."

Phil is watching me, warily, and I know he expects me to say something terrible, but I lean down and kiss my grandfather's white forehead and tell him he looks wonderful.

"Thank you, dear," he says, clearing his throat. I am above him, looking down at his bushy eyebrows and furrowed brow, his thin, white hair brushed neatly back. The hair is like a baby's now, and I touch the top of his head, smoothing the hair back. He looks up and says again, "Thank you, dear."

Phil says, "So, how long was your trip?"

"How long was it?"

He laughs. "I'm sorry. I wanted to ask how your trip was and how long you could stay, and I guess my mind merged the two thoughts."

"She's just here the week," Dad says.

I nod. Phil smiles and sips his drink. He is so at ease with himself that he can say anything, do anything, seemingly without embarrassment. I watch him walk by Dad and pat him on the shoulder as he moves to sit down. He pulls his slacks up slightly before he sits, then he places his drink on the coffee table and leans back, crossing his legs. He is self-assured, content.

Dad sits next to him. He is much shorter than Phil, and I am again surprised by this. All my life he has seemed tall to me, and each time I see him next to a taller man, it momentarily astonishes me. Also, it produces a sense of failure that I cannot explain. It is as though seeing him as he actually is destroys something essential in my memory.

"You want something to drink?" Phil says.

Dad shakes his head, staring at his father. I ask for a glass of wine.

"Honey?" Phil hollers.

"Dottie's here?" I say, and as I do, Phil's wife comes in from the kitchen. She has put on so much weight since the last time I saw her, I almost don't recognize her. She is wearing a jersey with a piano keyboard across the front, blue shorts, and white tennis shoes. She hugs me, takes my arms and holds them out away from me as though she is spreading a curtain, and then she scrutinizes me from head to toe.

"You are so beautiful, young lady."

"I'm not a young lady anymore," I say.

She hugs me again. "It's so good to see you."

I don't know what else to say. She looks like a soft, incredibly puffed version of her earlier self. When Phil first married her, she was very attractive. Her eyes were naturally dark. She had finely shaped lips, a nearly perfect nose, a delicate jaw. She was very petite and almost fragile. Now, she looks a little beset and imprisoned—as though her body has absorbed a portion of the atmosphere and might burst any minute.

"Come on in the kitchen," she says. "Let's get caught up."

I am reluctant to follow her out of the room, but I do it. The backs of her legs are mottled with little blue patterns.

In the kitchen, she wants to know all about my new husband. I tell her what I think she wants to hear: that I met him in guardedly romantic circumstances—a quiet dinner on a mutual friend's houseboat—and that he is a good man who does not drink. To impress her, I tell her that when he walks past the dryer he checks to see if there are dry clothes in there and, if he finds some, he takes them out and folds them right there.

Dottie is amazed. "I can see you really love him," she says.

I smile, thinking of him. I don't know, even now, if I love

him. I sometimes wish there were a blood test you could take, or something, to tell you if you're in love or not. What I do love about Gordon is I think I can trust him. I try not to think about the ways he misses the mark. There are plenty of times when I don't think about him at all.

Dottie tells me about Phil's latest successes. "He might end up in Washington," she says, thrilled at the possibility. "He's gotten so good at labor law, and now with a new administration, there's talk."

"That would be nice," I say.

By this time, Dottie has poured me a glass of white wine. She is mixing the other drinks when I become conscious of the laughter in the other room.

"They're telling stories again," Dottie says.

During my second glass of wine, Robert shows up. He is alone and not happy. I know when I see him that my father and Phil have not come here only to visit. They would not have gotten Robert to join them simply for old-time's sake. Something is going to happen. I think my grandfather senses it, too. "What are you doing here on a weekend?" he says.

"Just came to say hello," Robert says, offering his hand.

The old man looks at it for a moment, then he waves it away. "You're out on your boat."

"I usually am," Robert sighs.

"Why aren't you out there?"

Robert looks at my father and Phil. "I had to come for the big powwow."

Grandfather appears concerned. He frowns and regards Phil with curiosity. "What's going on?"

"Nothing," Phil says.

I walk into Uncle Robert's view, but he says nothing to me. He smiles briefly and then sits down. He is wearing white shorts and a white shirt with blue pockets. "What's everybody drinking?"

Dottie offers him a whiskey sour and he takes it. "I'll just mix myself another one," she says, retreating to the kitchen. I know she wants me to go with her, but I am too curious. I walk over to the wing chair by the entrance and sit down. I am across from my grandfather, my father and Phil are on a couch to his left, and Robert is sitting on the love seat to his right. The sun makes angles across the room. In the slanted light, my grandfather looks a little bit like Goya's vision of Saturn devouring one of his sons. His eyes are wide and his mouth is working.

But nothing happens. Phil starts telling another story. It is one about Robert. "We were drinking beer at the beach one night, talking about the sand crabs, the way they dig themselves instantly into the sand as soon as the water washes them up, and I told Robert that once, when I was in Ocean City, me and a few friends got up real early to watch the sun rise."

Dottie comes in with another whiskey sour and sits on the arm of the couch next to Phil. "Did I miss anything?" she says.

"Be quiet," Phil says. He looks at her momentarily, smiles, pats her knee, then goes on. "I told Robert that in the morning, when the world is lighting up but the sun hasn't peeked over the horizon yet, the sand crabs are all sort of hypnotized by the weak light and they don't try to hide."

Grandfather laughs, but it turns into a cough. It is really loud. He takes a white handkerchief out of his pocket and wipes his face with it, and then Phil goes on. "I told him they don't try to hide, that you can pick them up and hold them in your hand, and he wanted to try it in the morning. Then I told him that sometimes me and my friends would put the sand crabs into a small cup, half filled with beer. We'd let them swim around for a bit until they were good and drunk and then, just before the sun made its appearance, we'd pour them out on the sand. I said they were so drunk and confused that they would write their names in the sand. They write names like Tiki and Kiki. And Robert thinks about this for a while and then he says, 'They don't *know* they're writing their names in the sand.' "

Everybody laughs again. I am stricken by how odd my father's family is. They never talk about anything, really. Their way of relating to one another is to tell stories, or stupid jokes. Although my father laughs with them, he is always strangely quiet in these circumstances. I've watched him with his brothers, and sometimes he's tried to say something, and I've wanted him to, but he is drowned out by Phil or Robert or even Grandfather. It is almost as if they have heard all of Dad's stories and have found them unworthy.

When the laughter dies down a bit, Robert begins a story about my father. How when they were children they used to go swimming at a rock quarry in northern Maryland called Sylvan Dell. The rock quarry was a huge place, with deep, cold water, and there was a place there where you could jump from a rock wall more than a hundred feet into the black water below. When he was a senior in high school, Phil used to jump from there. He interrupts Robert to say, "It was like flying. I'd go all the way to the bottom and touch cold stone." He explains to us that he was everybody's hero because of those "giant leaps." At the time, my father was only nine years old, but one day he claimed that he wanted to make the jump.

"We all know Dad," Robert says. "The family rule was, if you got up on a diving board or climbed up on a swing or a slide or whatever, you were going off. There wasn't any changing your mind and climbing back down."

My grandfather seems to chuckle at this.

"So Shaver gets up there and spreads his arms, and then he freezes."

Phil is laughing. "He looked like he was being crucified on an invisible cross."

"He sounded like the Fly. 'Help me, help me.' " Robert's squeaky imitation makes even me laugh.

"And then," Robert says, "Dad goes up there next to him and

tells him he has to make the jump."

"The look on Shaver's face." Phil pushes my father, laughing.

Dad does not look at me, but there is a smile on his face that seems tense and frozen, and I know he is pretending to be amused. "I think I'll have a drink now, Dottie," he says.

"I'll get it," I tell him.

"Then," Robert says, "all the way back down from that cliff, he walked behind Dad chattering like a little monkey."

"That's right," Phil laughs. "He wouldn't stop talking."

"Just get me a beer," Dad says.

My grandfather laughs at Robert's story, and Dad looks away, seems to be staring into the space between all of them, waiting. I walk past him and on into the kitchen.

While I'm pouring my father's beer, I think I might start to cry. I wish he would sit up more, stop holding his hands together in his lap while Robert and Phil tell stories about him. Also, I realize, he would not seem so incomplete if my mother were here, loving him.

Dottie comes in behind me. "Oh, those men," she says. "They're so funny."

I don't say anything to her.

"Is anything wrong, dear?"

"I just miss my husband," I tell her.

"God love ya," she says.

I take my father's beer and walk back into the living room. Phil is telling another story. At first I don't listen to it, but as I hand the beer to my father, the look on his face stops me. He has the appearance of a little boy caught in a lie. And then I realize that Uncle Phil is telling the story of the encore fish. "So I waited until Shaver was in the cabin, and I took the fish out of the cooler and put it back on his line a fourth time."

My grandfather is laughing so hard Phil has to stop and wait for him.

"Four times he reeled in the same damned fish," Phil says.

"Shaver thought he was going to empty that lake."

Dad looks at his beer, shakes his head. He glances over at his father and then briefly at me. When his eyes meet mine, his self-possession falters and I know he does not want to be where I can see his face.

When Phil is finished I don't say anything.

"'This one's a little sluggish,'" Phil says again, still laughing.

My father will not look at me. Just now, he seems forlorn and hopelessly lost. I want him to know it doesn't matter to me. But there is nothing I can say to him. When everyone notices that Dad is not laughing, a brief and awful silence overtakes us.

Then Phil says, "One time, my Ford LTD station wagon dieseled backward up a hill and out of a 7- Eleven parking lot while I was inside buying beer."

I don't want to be there anymore, or hear any more stories.

It goes on for a long time. Gradually, the laughter dies down, and then in the quiet that follows, Phil suddenly begins telling my grandfather what the purpose of this meeting is: to let him know that he will have to move into a home with a private room where he will be taken care of every day. He will have the best care available, and he won't want anything and he won't have to do anything. The home he will move to is very near, so his sons will always be close by.

Grandfather takes this news surprisingly well, as though he expected it. Dottie whispers to me that she thinks it's because he's given up, but I'm not even sure he understands what is happening to him. As we are leaving, Grandfather says to me, "You take care of yourself, Marie."

Dad says, "Marie passed away. This is Nicole, your granddaughter."

"Oh," grandfather says.

I kiss his coarse cheek and he smiles. "It will be all right," I tell him.

"What?" His shaggy brow twitches. "What will be all right?"

I shrug. "The move and everything."

"It's bullshit, Honey," he says. "You know it?"

"Yes," I say, and kiss him again.

"It's all just bullshit."

I pat the side of his face.

"Good night, Marie," he says.

On the ride home, Dad has nothing to say. I watch the streetlights racing past, and I realize that I am acquainted with the future. I know it as though it has already happened. I will go home next week, gradually take up my life there again. Gordon will never want children, and I will come to see that he is probably right. Things will work out for the best. It will be difficult to save the kind of money I will need to return to Baltimore any time soon.

Perhaps in the years ahead I will find a way to come back to Baltimore three or four more times. Meanwhile, the years will pile up, secretly, on us. I'll send my father Christmas cards. Birthday cards. Father's Day cards. He will call me on my birthday. In spite of my best hopes, I know that most of my time with Dad will be over the telephone. When we talk, he will tell me stories—perhaps even the story of the encore fish. We will have many conversations as the Thanksgiving holidays and Christmas seasons pass, year after year, and then one day I'll get a call from Annette or Richard, and I will know what they have to tell me before they say it.

All this time, I will hate the distances we create for ourselves in this small world.

Siobhan Dowd, program director of PEN American Center's Freedom-to-Write Committee, writes this column regularly, alerting readers to the plight of writers around the world who deserve our awareness and our writing action.

Silenced Voice: Doan Viet Hoat

by Siobhan Dowd

In an open letter to Vietnam's communist rulers, the writer Doan Viet Hoat called on his government to make some revolutionary decisions: "Release all political detainees," he advised. "Implement freedom of speech, press, and religion. Organize free and fair elections. Only by doing this can our country be brought out of its present deadlock and integrated into the world community. The survival of the communist party should no longer be allowed to take precedence over the national destiny and the people's welfare."

Doan Viet Hoat

Unfortunately, Doan's audacious advice caused him to be dubbed a "bad element" in Vietnam's tightly controlled official press and earned him a staggering fifteen-year prison term—one of the stiffest ever handed down to a writer anywhere.

Glimmer Train Stories, Issue 11, Summer 1994

Doan, fifty-one, is no criminal. He has devoted his life to Buddhism, study, and teaching. He graduated from Saigon University in 1965, taught English in a school in the Mekong Delta, and then became a personnel advisor at Van Hanh University, a Buddhist institution in Saigon. In 1967, having won a scholarship from the Asia Foundation, he went to the U.S., where he received a Ph.D. in education at Florida State University. On his return in 1971, he became vice-president of Van Hanh University.

After the fall of Saigon in 1975, the Socialist Republic of Vietnam was declared, and the new government called on intellectuals from the south to enroll in a course of "reeducation." Many of those who refused were arrested. The "reeducation" consisted of being sent to remote, harsh work camps for years on end, without charge or trial. The government typically defended its behavior by claiming that the camps represented an act of mercy: by rights, they said, all their inmates should have been executed for war crimes.

Doan had the option of leaving the country in 1975. According to his wife, Tran Thi Thuc, he stayed because he had faith in the new regime and wanted to participate in the rebuilding of his devastated country. However, the government, frowning on Buddhism generally, and on Van Hanh University in particular, arrested Doan for "reeducation" and he remained incarcerated for twelve years.

Doan was released in 1988 during a brief political thaw which many commentators hailed as the beginning of a Vietnamese *glasnost*. New writers emerged, experimenting with poetry, novels, and essays that questioned the revolution and analyzed afresh the aftermath of the war. Doan was no exception: as well as teaching English at the University of Agriculture and Forestry, he founded a group called Freedom Forum, along with a samizdat journal of the same name that consisted of typewritten sheets, copied and passed from hand to hand by its readers.

Advocating political and economic reform, it contained essays by Doan and other writers in his circle, and articles taken from foreign newspapers or written by Vietnamese living abroad.

The authorities became aware of its existence only in 1990, when one of *Freedom Forum*'s members brought copies to Canada. These found their way into a Vietnamese-language publication in the U.S., and soon after came a crackdown on all those associated with Doan's group.

On November 17, 1990, Doan himself was arrested at his house in the Phu Nhuan district of Saigon and taken to a local jail. Six months elapsed before his wife and children were informed of his whereabouts.

A sure indication that the trial would go against Doan and the other intellectuals arrested with him was the appearance of an article in Saigon's *Giai Phong* newspaper, which used the words "reactionary," "surreptitious," and "demagogic" to paint Doan as the mastermind of a nefarious plot to overthrow the government. According to the paper:

> Doan Viet Hoat's group feverishly pressed forward with establishing a political organization to operate in secret. The most important political ploy they chose was the argument for "democracy." They lost no time in drafting an "appeal to all people to struggle for democracy," which fully and clearly exposed their sinister intention and dark and crazy ambition in four stages of action ... Doan Viet Hoat sought out a number of people who had once served in the former Saigon puppet army and administration; the entire plot, led by Doan Viet Hoat, was uncovered and smashed in 1990.

Doan's wife responded by writing to the authorities, complaining in soft, diplomatic language that her husband's guilt appeared to have been decided before his trial—in violation of the Vietnamese constitution. However, she received no reply. In March 1993, Doan was convicted of attempting to overthrow the government.

Early in 1994, PEN heard that Doan had been transferred to Xuan Phuoc Prison in Phu Yen City, some six hundred and fifty kilometers from Saigon, where his family lives. No reasons were given for the transfer, but because of the distance, his wife has had difficulty visiting him and giving him the medication he needs for a serious kidney ailment. If Doan serves his sentence in full, he will be in his seventies on his release, and he will have spent over half his life behind bars.

Please send polite letters calling for Doan Viet Hoat's unconditional release to:

His Excellency Do Muoi
Secretary General
The Vietnamese Communist Party
HANOI, SOCIALIST REPUBLIC OF VIETNAM

A single sheet of paper in a standard envelope requires fifty cents postage.

Thanks are due to Asia Watch for information contained in this article, and for the translation of the quotes from Vietnamese.

Christine Liotta

I fall in love every autumn. Even as far back as my first Halloween (which is still my favorite holiday), I think I was already beginning to fall in love with pumpkin weather: the clear, crisp, true autumnal sunlight that makes everything—buildings and trees in particular—seem permanently etched in space, and the colors all around growing deeper and richer, more themselves it seems to me. Over the years, I've noticed that my strongest impressions of the world—and many short stories—have been born in the frost and shadows of autumn.

Christine Liotta was born in New York City and grew up on Long Island. After receiving a B.F.A. from Carnegie-Mellon University, where she studied painting and writing, she continued graduate-level work in creative writing at City College of New York. She makes her living as a writer, editor, and proofreader, and has published fiction, poetry, and journalism in many arts and literary journals.

Liotta is working on a collection of stories to be titled *What Is Given*, and renovating her loft in Long Island City, New York.

CHRISTINE LIOTTA

Counted Blessings

Fall

My parents named me January, in honor of the first successful sex they had. True enough, since I was born in October, but I often wonder to myself how great a misfortune it is to have been christened with such an idiotic name. I wonder if it is worse than having merely a boring name. Take *Keith,* for example, the name of the man I live with. Although not nearly as absurd as January, *Keith* possesses no richness, no sultry subtlety. *Keith* just kind of lies there, dead as driftwood. On the other hand, and I am always careful to look at both sides of any given situation, the name *Shazam* does the man justice. I've called Keith Shazam for three years now, and I suppose, therefore, that I am responsible for that gradually taking the place of his given name. But it quite suits him. While *Keith* gets caught in the throat and on the teeth, *Shazam* floats exuberantly and effortlessly past the lips. It means the good guy in the movies. Instead of his name merely meaning driftwood, it now means superhero.

That said, I ought to tell you that I've lived with this name for twenty-five years now (and with Keith for two), and though I've often thought of changing it, I haven't come up with anything better that I could imagine sticking with for life. If I had to be

Glimmer Train Stories, Issue 11, Summer 1994

named after a month, I would have preferred something dark and autumnal, like October Apple or September Rain. Because January expresses no mystery, no roundness or ripeness, nothing at all. My parents, in their witless celebration, hadn't even thought to cleverly pair it with a middle name.

"Why did you do it?" I ask my mother.

"I thought it was a sure way to get the family together." She is referring to the fiftieth birthday party she has thrown for herself. Guest list: two widowed aunts and myself. My father doesn't count as a guest as he already lives there.

My parents have moved temporarily into a sales-model apartment because their new condominium has not been completely built yet, although it is two months past the move-in date. The bind is that my parents sold their previous house, and the new owners already moved in two months ago, so my parents are left between homes at the moment. The building company is housing them here in the sales model, rent-free, as compensation. Every room has mirrors on the walls, and on the mirrors are small cardboard signs which say "optional." The water faucets are all labeled with warnings, and the furniture is plastic lawn chairs and a redwood set, as the real furniture has been packed away until they can move into the real condominium. The builders promise that this should only be about three more weeks, when the plumbing and heating systems are working properly and all the wood finishes are done. One entire room is filled to the ceiling with cardboard boxes, waiting to be unpacked.

Despite these less than ideal conditions, my parents always astonish me with their ability to adapt. Every light in the apartment is on as I watch my mother's strong fingers rip into the raw chicken on the Formica countertop, tearing it into individual-sized dinner portions. The sleeves of her white silk blouse are rolled up to her elbows. She stops for a moment to fix her slip, then continues tearing at the meat. It seems a motherly thing to do, like the way mother animals behave on "Wild Kingdom."

The blouse was a birthday gift from me. I stole it from Foxx's, the department store on Fifth Avenue where I work. This stealing is something I've only recently acquired a knack for, and which I'll explain later. For now, let it suffice to say that I am an underpaid customer-service rep and display artist. I also stole the pearl earrings my mother is wearing.

I am sitting at the other end of the counter, slicing vegetables for the salad, when my mother asks: "How is Keith?" She refuses to use *Shazam,* the more affectionate name. She tears off a leg from the chicken carcass and it makes a horrible sound, like something being stretched beyond its limits.

"Shazam is well," I say, slicing a carrot in response to her chicken ripping. "He says Happy Birthday to you."

"It's a pity he never learned to speak for himself."

"I've already explained that he had to work late again last night," I say, and realize that, not only am I defending him once again, but that I am gesticulating with a carrot as I speak. "Shazam is a very serious and sensitive man," I continue. "Did you know that he cries every time he hears Frank Sinatra sing 'Some Enchanted Evening'?"

"Why no," says my mother, backing down.

"Both versions," I add triumphantly.

After dinner and cake at the picnic table set up in the dining area, I paint my mother's fingernails Coral Frost (from Foxx's, naturally) before catching the train back to the city, back to Shazam. We don't really live in the city, but on Roosevelt Island, which, at the time it was rebuilt, was designed to be a model of modern life and yet still have the feel of a small town in the shadow of Manhattan. Roosevelt Island is a thin sliver of land floating halfway between Manhattan Island and Long Island. It has a long history. At one time, criminals were exiled to

Roosevelt Island, and the mentally ill. Perhaps it is the perfect place for us to live. The view of the Manhattan skyline at night can't be beat.

As I leave, my mother is in the middle of the living room, surrounded on three sides by optional mirrors, practicing her golf swing with the new driver my father has given her. I look past her for a moment, out the window at the man-made lake in the backyard, with its continually spouting, illuminated fountain in the center. At the front door, my father removes a brand-new, crisp, one hundred-dollar bill from his wallet and folds it into my palm. "Get a new job," he says.

It will be raining. It will just be beginning to get dark in the city, rush hour perhaps. I'll be standing in the doorway of that delicatessen with the varnished loaves of bread in the window. I'll be wearing a red scarf, but I'm sure I will recognize you first. You'll be standing in a phone booth for shelter. Hey baby, whaddaya say? It seems we're the only two people in town without umbrellas. Your suede jacket is darkly spotted from the rain, and a small trickle of water runs down your arm, but you don't even notice. Hey wait, can't I walk with you for a bit? You're heading west, away from me, your jacket meshing with the wet bricks of the building behind you.

Sometimes I must remind myself that I am a woman, that I am young still, still attractive, that I am quite average in almost every way except for my ability to lie. I have always been a liar. That is not to say that I am incapable of telling the truth; quite the opposite, I can do that just as easily. But lying, as I learned early on, is a much more useful skill—not only concealing those annoying lapses in emotional response, but in all levels of interpersonal relationships, it is more valuable than the art of conversation (though these two are closely related), or even letter writing. Besides, people only really listen to what they want to hear in the first place. It is a rare occasion when someone takes a genuine interest in what you think to be true. For example, Shazam thinks that I enjoy baseball, Bob Dylan, reading newspapers, and that I actually like the four miserable cats that live with us. I don't. Shazam buys one daily newspaper, one weekly paper, and three Sunday papers, which then grow into towers in every corner of our apartment until he takes them to be recycled once a month. When we were on holiday in France years ago (only two, but it feels like ten), Shazam bought a paper every day, though he can't even read French, just to have the feel of a newspaper in his hands.

I prefer to sit down together to watch the "Nando Corbett" show, the newest of those talk shows dealing with the decidedly current and burning issues of our time. Shazam and I do this faithfully each evening when we get home from work. Today the topic is venereal diseases, and one doctor estimates that thirty-one million Americans are afflicted with genital herpes. Shazam and I smile. We laugh over it. I say that I'd sue him. Shazam asks me one of his famous morbid sports trivia questions: "What Brooklyn Dodger star catcher was paralyzed in a plane crash?"

Shazam sells refrigerator parts for a living, and travels frequently for his job. He's been having an affair with a flight attendant from Washington, D.C., which I've known about for six months. Shazam says it's over between them, but he is a liar, too. He has learned this from me. That is how I can tell.

The women who shop at Foxx's wear lots of jewelry, no less than three gold necklaces each. Real gold. And they are all so thin that it is impossible to even venture a guess as to their ages. Nilda and I, as the two senior customer-service reps, are faced with scores of these gold-throated toothpicks each day in our accursed department. "My husband bought me this and it doesn't quite fit... It doesn't go with our drapes... It doesn't go with our life." If it is not enough that I seem to have a metabolic reaction to ramblings of this sort, the whole while I must wear a badge that proclaims "Service With A Smile," which, of course, has my unfortunate appellation boldly embossed on the red strip of adhesive plastic, for all to see.

Leo, my boss, knows that in another of my incarnations I had once had artistic aspirations, and so gives me a creative outlet by allowing me to help in window display and dressing the models in Foxx fashions. No extra money. Leo has a large, uneven patch of gray hair that looks as if someone dipped a hand in a canister of flour and then smacked him in the back of the head.

Things to do today: wash dishes
go to bank
birthday card for Mom
cat litter
cat food
train tokens
work

By eight a.m., Shazam is dressed and ready for work. I've watched him secretly—watched him sitting in the dusty corner by the window tying his shoes, combing his hair, looking for his cigarettes. "Where are my cigarettes?" he asks. "January, have you seen my cigarettes? Jan?"

I gesture no, turning my head back and forth against the pillow.

"Dammit," he says.

Dammit, I mimic in my head. The blanket and sheets are suffused with our smells. The truth is I've hidden them.

a) because they're bad for you,

b) because I want them for myself,

c) because you might stay around a while longer looking for them.

I wonder if Miss Washington, D.C., also hides his cigarettes so that he won't leave so abruptly. I wonder whether she calls him Keith or has some other cute nickname. Sometimes I think,

How could he? How dare he?

After Shazam leaves for work, I lie in bed and practice saying his name, his real name, Keith. I say it over and over, in three parts, like exercising: 1) k

2) ee

3) th

I practice the woodenness of it. I'm not sure what I'm practicing for, as I lie here with the sunlight slashing through the blinds, already a half hour late for work. Our neighbor begins practicing his saxophone early today and I can hear quite clearly his squeaking version of "When the Saints Go Marching In." He can hardly play at all without hitting a wrong or flat note, but for some reason the tune always cheers me.

I never get to see the apartment like this. It feels like a Sunday afternoon, flooded with golden light. But this effect lasts only briefly, about twenty minutes, the time it takes the sun to rise above the angle where it comes in through the blinds. The chairs seem to be angry, and the dishes. In the mirror, my face is swollen. I look like a lizard. A reptile. A customer-service reptile.

On some days, commuters emerge from the subway system like brightly colored tennis balls from an automatic server, into the brisk city morning. Other days, as if by mutual agreement, no one keeps pace with anyone else. We are as if lost in the various rhythms of our own thoughts, causing collisions with our umbrellas, not looking up, even as we cross the street. Today is one of those days.

On the train, five women, including myself, stand in a tight circle around the same chrome post, clutching it ridiculously, as if it belonged to us, as if it were something we really wanted, a magic broomstick or a pointed javelin.

The woman directly across from me looks as if she is smelling garbage. The woman to her right looks as if she will burst into tears at any moment. Another appears to be blind in one eye. I look away, into the corner, where a man and woman seated side by side appear to be speaking to one another. After long observation, I realize that they are not speaking at all. The train grinds to a stop and the conductor says, "As the Beverly Hillbillies once said: 'Y'all come back now, you hear?' Step lively."

A man on the street catches my eye. He forms an imaginary gun from his thumb and forefinger and points it directly at my head, straight between my eyes. He pulls the trigger and at the same time makes an exploding noise. In the confusion and dread of wondering whether I have really been shot in the head, I stop dead in my tracks. I realize I have not been shot. For the second time today, and it is still early, I bite the insides of my cheeks to keep from crying. The taste of blood in my mouth reminds me of someone I once knew. At work I attribute my lateness to a burst pipe in the bathroom. Later, I slip another white blouse into my bag. This one is for myself.

Winter

I've come down with a slight cold and do not feel like going to work today. But to call in sick again would be a bit extreme, even for me. I call my boss. "Hello, Leo? It's January."

"No it isn't. It's still December." He laughs at his same old joke.

"I'm sorry, but I can't come in today."

"Are you still not feeling well?"

"I was feeling much better, but actually, I was moving my car this morning to the alternate side of the street and I got hit by a bus."

"Oh my God! Are you all right?"

"I'm okay. My back and neck are a little bit whiplashed. Can you believe the idiocy of these bus drivers? And it was a school bus no less, with children in it for Chrissakes."

Leo says that I should take lots of hot baths and not to worry about anything.

When Shazam comes home from work we watch the "Nando Corbett" show together. Nando Corbett is a man with a name. Its simple sharpness pops out of one's mouth practically without effort. Not only are his questions to his guests fair-minded and politically correct, but he manages to always get to the heart of the issue, even with the most uncooperative guests or studio audience. I love watching him take control of a discussion and extracting the truth of the matter, like a perfect tooth from an old woman's mouth. Once, I even heard him say "horseshit" on television.

Today's segment is about people with facial disfigurements. They talk about how difficult it has been for them to overcome the odds and lead a normal life. They talk about being stared at all the time. They don't say "handicapped," they say "physically challenged." We're people in here, they say. Images of infants born without noses or eyes flash on the television screen. Shazam turns to me and says, "What New York Yankee captain lost his life in an airplane crash in 1976?"

In the evening, my cold gets worse. I remember reading somewhere that all disease is actually love transformed. Shazam is good to me when I am sick. He buys tissues, aspirin, juice, and cough drops. He slices vegetables for dinner and puts up some lentil soup. We sit across the table from one another, it seems the first time in a long time, and I remember how much I like the way the hair tucks behind his ears under his cap. I reach across the table and clutch his hand as if he belonged to me. "I've had a dream," I say. "A dream that you would leave me. It's okay."

Under the table, the cats weave between our legs, and I see that Shazam has fed them my leftover spaghetti. I don't know whether to feel insulted or honored. "Look, Jan," he starts, but then changes his mind. I see that it's D.C. again. "January, you're really a wonderful person. You're intelligent and sweet and beautiful. You deserve much better than this."

"What are you talking about?" I ask. I never think of myself as any of those things. I wonder why, if I am all those things to him, why doesn't he love me?

"I consider the fact that you don't like baseball to be a major problem in our relationship," he says, taking his hand back, putting it under the table.

"What about the fact that we don't have sex anymore?" I ask, determined to have our problems reflect something more significant than a disagreement about baseball.

"We have sex," he says quickly.

I pause for a minute, perplexed. How could two reasonable people look at the exact same thing and then voice two extremely different, in fact, opposing, points of view? For weeks I have begun to feel unnecessary, obsolete, like something that no longer fits, a tight bra, a tight shoe waiting to be cast off at the end of a long day, an alpaca scarf in summer. Shazam excuses himself from the table to pay the bills. I am still sitting in the kitchen while Shazam makes his evening phone calls. His soft murmurings through the closed door are barely audible. "I am over here," I whisper to myself. "I overhear you."

Later, in the middle of the night, I wake from feverish dreams of boiling oceans and slip out of bed. Shazam is asleep, the cats are asleep. In my nightgown, I creep on tiptoe down the darkened hallway to the bathroom, and I feel like the heroine of some television horror film—Karen Black or Mia Farrow. I keep thinking: Someone is going to kill me. Someone is going to kill me.

About an hour later, Shazam finds me sitting on the edge of the bathtub, a wet washcloth across my forehead. He collects my

snotty tissues, carries us back to bed, my body and me, and holds us tight. It is as though he is carrying me across Nebraska, my superhero.

Words that should be stricken from the English language:

1. surge
2. relieve
3. relief
4. persevere
5. perhaps
6. hygiene
7. outrageous
8. artist
9. mind-set

You again. I've heard you whistling all day. At first, it sounds powerful and loud, like a siren or a warning. You blow three long notes in a row. Each starts at a high pitch and volume and slowly descends.

I know you are trying to tell me something. I hear you whistling in the subway station, the library, the coffee shop. Maybe it is a common symptom of men in your condition. Sickness? Delirium? Lust? Some form of consumption? It must be you watching me cross the street, put down a steaming cup of coffee, check out a book. Always smiling to yourself, and always, always blowing hot air between your lips.

Once every nine nights, Shazam and I feel in love again. There's nothing better than seeing him licking the clam sauce I've just made off his lips and hearing him say he never wants his spaghetti any other way. Or when we're making cookies with Dylan crooning on in the background about being tangled or tied up. With Shazam's stubble against my cheek, his hair curled in dark ringlets on the back of his neck, it seems so easy.

I stole him a telescope from Foxx's as a Christmas present. It is rather an expensive one, but since he is taking an astronomy class at the high school Tuesday nights, he really needs his own telescope. I wrap it carefully in copies of my résumé then I cut out pictures from magazines and tape them on. When he comes home from work, we sit on the floor and make Christmas cards together to send to our families and friends, to the beautiful music of "When the Saints Go Marching In" on saxophone.

This evening, Nando Corbett is discussing the shortest marriages in history. None of the guests on the show had marriages that lasted for more than six months, though the general average is about three weeks. One guest met a man at work and married him one week later. They went out to dinner to celebrate after the ceremony. During dinner, the new groom had a change of heart and, immediately following dessert, he drove her straight back to her parents' house. He said her parents had bribed him into it.

In the middle of the show, my mother calls. I feel myself becoming curt with her because she should know by now not to call when our show is on. But she is furious that we are going to Shazam's parents' house for Christmas dinner. I try to get off the phone, say I'm in the middle of something, but she presses the matter.

"Did you know that his parents own a Matisse?" I ask.

"Why, no," says my mother, backing down.

"And a Miró," I add proudly.

Counted blessings:

1. a rich fantasy life
2. decapitated Santa heads on wall in the bank
3. I have two arms and two legs.
4. My parents love me.
5. "When the Saints Go Marching In" on saxophone.

Futile gestures:

1. adding salt when boiling water
2. the man on the subway station platform opening and closing his umbrella six or seven times in rapid succession in order to dry it
3. holding hands

Leo has given me the day after Christmas off, even though it is the busiest day of the year in my department with all the returns and complaints. We visit Shazam's family in Virginia, where I am introduced as "Keith's girl," and we all watch television together. First, we tune in to a talk show hosted by a competitor of Nando Corbett, discussing, of all things, genital herpes. After that, we watch a videotape of one of Shazam's sisters giving birth to her first child. Shazam and I hold hands tightly. I tell him that I'd kill him. His mother and sisters look at me, then at him, then at me again. One of the sisters says, "Keith looks fine, but January's as white as a ghost!" I smile politely. We have sausage and hard-boiled eggs for dinner.

Shazam loves the telescope and, when we get back home, we relegate it to a place of honor in the apartment: by the window, atop a newspaper tower. We don't use it to spy on the neighbors, but only to get a glimpse out of this apartment and into the night sky. I try to ask him a question he would find interesting, something about constellations, but he isn't listening.

"We've declined," I announce.

"What?"

"If I say 'We've declined,' would you think I meant we've been reduced, or that we've said 'no' to something? Would one be the result of the other?"

I'm peering at him through the distorted glass of the telescope. He looks ludicrous, sitting there in his underwear and red socks, reading the Sunday paper, smoking a big fat cigar. The cigars are a Christmas gift from Miss D.C., which have appeared in the apartment somewhat mysteriously. I am wearing the blue sweater Shazam gave me for Christmas.

"You know," I say. "You have such a way of making me miserable."

He finally looks up over the top of his newspaper. "I do?" he asks, disbelievingly. "Me?"

I realize I don't talk much about life B.S. (before Shazam), but I will move to another subject. I've begun to steal from Foxx's on a nearly daily basis. I don't feel very guilty about it; in fact, I rather enjoy it. Nilda knows, but she and I have an understanding. In an almost competitive way, she asks me each day if I've stolen something, while I ask her each day if she's taken any substances. What I do is, every time I go to dress the display models, I bring *two* of everything—one for the model and one for my toolbox. Plus some other incidentals that I need. At the employee entrance, the security guards take a quick peek into my pocketbook, but never, never look in my toolbox.

I've begun to keep a list of all the things I've stolen from Foxx's and how much they cost:

shirt	$44.00
telescope	$399.99
musk	$16.00
Aqua Ban	$8.00
hair clip	$13.50
earrings	$20.00
dress	$88.00
comb	$9.00
change purse	$78.00
underwear	$7.50
face mask	$15.00
can opener	$12.00

Lately, I think one of the security guards is on to me. This morning he mentioned how much he liked my new dress and asked if it was expensive. I said no. He even offered to help carry my toolbox, but I wouldn't let him touch it. I'm sure he won't say anything because he has a crush on me and wants to date me. I don't even think of him as a real security guard. He's never caught anyone with anything. He only got this job because his sister designs the bathing suits we sell.

Nilda and I go out to lunch at the coffee shop. Another of my habits these days is to see how long I can make one cheeseburger and one beer last. So far, one hour, twenty-two minutes. Nilda complains bitterly about her time-share on Long Island. She talks about her wedding plans. She clasps her hands together and flashes her engagement ring. She tells me her weekend plans but doesn't invite me along. Instead, she asks if I stole today. She looks at my toolbox, my eyes. When I begin to cry, she asks what's wrong.

"Nothing," I say. "Nothing."

"It's okay, Jan," she says as I notice a teardrop rolling down my name tag, which I had forgotten to remove, still pinned to my blouse. "We're family here," she says.

She gives me half a Quaalude. I pay for lunch.

Spring

Shazam has accepted a job transfer to Washington, D.C., and will be moving the first of May, when our lease runs out. I will not be accompanying him. We split up like this: I woke up one morning and, while I was still half asleep, made a phlegmatic egg and cheese sandwich, ate two bites of what did not stick to the frying pan, and then got nauseated and threw the rest in the trash. I had to go to work; he had to pay the bills.

"I'm leaving," he said, without looking up.

For a second, I thought he had said he was bleeding, and felt a momentary surge of relief.

"What will I say to my mother?"

"That's your problem."

We decided we will both be moving when the lease runs out next month.

When we finally come face to face, the blue-gray light will make everything look like a scene from Wuthering Heights. *We'll have to go out a lot, you and I, to wine and cheese places or quiet cafes. Would you like to go to a movie? Would you like to fuck for a while? Shall we tell each other our dreams? Shall we read to each other at night? Men of mystery can be so dreary.*

Reluctantly, and on a Thursday, I accept a date from the security guard at work. I tell Shazam that Nilda and I are going shopping. I don't even know why I bother lying about it. Maybe it is because the guard and I go to a baseball game, Shazam's domain. I dutifully fill in all the correct symbols on my scorecard, as Shazam taught me to do, and I think how proud he would be to see me do so. The security guard is not impressed. I look at him out of the corner of my eye. His profile is unflattering but strong, in a gangsterlike sort of way, if only he would close his mouth. He drops a hand to my shaven thigh. I ignore it.

After the game, he takes me to a sleazy Irish bar with tatty green vinyl seats and portraits of Lincoln and Washington on the walls. In another painting, a woman peers around the corner at a little girl and boy dancing or embracing. Our waitress wears a short skirt and a tired sweater which reveals her flesh-colored bra through the loose knitting. At the table next to us, someone asks, "Whatever happened to your edible underwear?"

Nothing on the menu appeals to me. "Get a burger," the security guard urges, "or a grilled cheese, a BLT."

The only thing I am certain of is that I do not want to eat with my hands. Imagining the luxury of a spoon, I order the soup, which turns out to be just a cup of broth with frozen vegetables wilting in it. He orders the turkey. I complain the whole time about the soup, the atmosphere, the paintings, the music, our jobs. I complain about everything, then apologize sweetly.

"You know what Thursday is, don't you?" he asks.

"Thursday is today."

"It's Anything Can Happen night. You'll see."

He offers me a mushroom from his plate, which I refuse. I'm playing my cards right.

suntan products	$24.00
shorts	$50.00
shorts	$25.00
shirt	$72.00
lighters	$6.00
massage brush	$19.00
hairbands	$3.00
bracelet	$36.00
gum/candy	$20.00
bathing suit	$90.00
blank tapes	$8.50

books	$24.00
conditioner	$6.00
bras	$60.00
sunglasses	$45.00

Shazam asks me to cut his hair. We step onto our fire escape and balance some wobbly chairs and a lamp. I snip the longish locks from his head and toss them over the rail. They float like confetti down the three flights onto the heads of a few scattered passersby in the street. I brush some of the clippings off his bare shoulders and into a plastic Baggie. On a nearby rooftop, a man and a woman in their underwear lie tanning themselves in yellow and green plastic lawn chairs, their bodies already dark and slick like packed plums. Their radio is blaring rap music from one of those stations at the bottom of the dial.

The scissors don't work so well, and it takes numerous hacks to remove one handful of hair from his head. He is determined to have it all go. All. I begin by making a braid, then cutting that off with one single cut of the scissors, and wrapping that, too, in a plastic Baggie. When the scissors become futile, I take the buzz shears to his head. Row by row, the coarse, uneven mat of hair becomes uniform in length and texture. The lamp suspended in the grates reflects light from the ends of his mutilated hairs, cut down like blades of grass. However, blades of grass have it pretty well, relatively. I guide the shears around his painfully conspicuous left ear and I realize that I have never seen his pink ears this exposed. The cats are purring and looking at themselves in the mirror I have dragged onto the fire escape. "Would you rather be Ted Bundy or Charles Manson?" I ask. He runs his palm across the top of his head. It is done.

Words I like:

1. shuttlecock
2. rogue

3. crackbrained
4. rasher
5. purblind
6. coffee cart
7. donut
8. obey (obedient)
9. relief
10. ditty bag
11. surge

Phrases:

1. Hello, my name is Miss Wonderful. Are you my husband?
2. Healthiness is better than sickness.
3. Laughter is better than crying.
4. dream turned to Hell
5. Small talk can be deadly.

In the middle of April I wake to frozen waffles, sour strawberries, and fried ham. I push it around with my knife and fork.

"I'm sorry," says Shazam. "It seems I'm always saying that to you."

"I dreamed of waiting on very long lines," I say. And then: "Why did I think we were any different?"

"I'm deeply sorry," he says.

I empty a full shaker of salt on the meal he's so sincerely prepared for me, saying, "Well well well. Well well well well well."

One of the cats, the tiger, jumps onto my lap. "Keith," I say quietly. Light glares off the utensils I am brandishing in both hands. "Get this thing off me before I impale it."

My opinions of people fluctuate daily. For example, the security guard starts to look not so bad after all, and, after three baseball games and Irish bars, I sleep with him. Three is usually a lucky number. When I get home, I soak my underwear in the bathroom sink. When he asks me out again, I refuse, and tell him he's a pig. In retaliation, he turns me in to Leo. I am immediately dismissed. The last thing I remember is arguing with a customer who was trying to return used dishes. I remember her looking at my badge and squinting to make out my name. "What is your name?" she asked.

"In case you can't read, it's January," I snapped. "As in the first month of the year."

I haven't said my own name out loud in such a long time. The customer's perfume hangs in the air as Leo touches my elbow, so tenderly it almost belies the fact that he is about to fire me.

"We need to talk," he says with a serious face I have never seen him use before. His mouth is pulled all the way across his face, where it makes deep creases on both sides of his chin. I think he wants to talk to me about my rudeness to the customer. "There are rumors that you've been less than honest here," he says slowly. His ears look folded, like little white-bread sandwiches. I don't try to deny anything. Leo is near tears. "This is like walking into a nightmare," he says, sighing. It is unclear whether Foxx's will press charges. All I know is that Nilda will get my job, including display privileges.

Later, in two separate phone calls, I explain to Shazam and to my parents that I've been set free like a helium balloon on a windy day.

1. My head is filled with a sensation which worries me.
2. Am I going to die soon?
3. high blood pressure?
4. smoking
5. why dizzy?
6. difficulty breathing/speaking
7. what now?
8. blood test/anemia

9. circulation (hands, feet, nose)

I can hardly stand to talk to people without beating them. I watch a great deal of television. Nando Corbett discusses feuding neighbors who turn one another's dogs loose, shine spotlights in each other's bedroom windows, choke each other's mothers-in-law. The news says that three swimmers have drowned because of tremendously strong riptides. A character on my favorite soap opera falls into a pool of quicksand and sinks very slowly, getting deeper before each commercial. Seconds before her head goes under, she is rescued. It is impossible to convey lifelong obsession on a soap opera, only a hysterical view of human life, a fantasy, a nonexistent status quo, and this very much agrees with me.

The summer, I know, will be hot and slow. I will spend it in my parents' condominium, thinking about looking for a new job and trying to forget. But, for now, we are here still, and our lives are once again filled with cardboard boxes, packing and unpacking, taking objects from dusty shelves and moving them to dusty boxes. Shazam's boxes are in the living room, mine in the kitchen. It's an incredible ritual, putting all your crusty belongings into cardboard boxes and moving to another place, a different box in which you will live, and take them all out again. The apartment seems suddenly to smell a bit moldy, like a hamper. I try to eradicate this by frying up some onions.

There is a storm coming this afternoon. Dark, thick clouds have rolled in from the west so quickly and the bright Sunday afternoon suddenly darkens while flashes of lightning rip through the pink sky and the rain comes down hard and fast. I feel as if I could actually live like this, with the feeling of being in the final moments.

The door opens and Shazam walks in. The optimistic smell of the onions seems to have no effect on him. He just says, "Hi."

His clothes are drenched through and he silently peels off all his wet clothes except his underwear, and stands very still, as if waiting. His sleek shadow almost moves me to tears. He goes over to the open window, leans over the wet windowsill, and looks out. Down below, people have come out of the shops on the street to look at the sky. Others are running to take cover. He turns and looks at me in the eerie light, and he sighs audibly. I walk toward him and, finally, he takes me in his arms.

We stand by the window, right in front of it, embracing as if it really is the end of time. Rain pours down, steady and hard, splashing against my back and legs, my clothes becoming wet, clinging. I have a strong desire to peel them off, like a dead skin. But, instead, we back away from one another.

"Oh, January," Shazam sighs.

"I know it's not a particularly interesting name," I say, defending my epithet. "It's not wonderful or subtle, but neither is Keith. Does anyone's name really do them justice? Except for Nando Corbett and maybe Vladimir Nabokov, who'd be willing to say their name does them justice? Who? Yes, January is a completely idiotic name, but I've been living inside this name for twenty-five years now, and I still haven't gotten used to it. I suppose that's one reason to have kids—to give them a better name than you got. What's her name, anyway?"

"What?" Shazam asks, startled.

"What's her name?"

"Who?"

"You know who. What's her name?"

He says my name twice more, as if he'd been practicing all his life. I can see his face in the light of the window, and it seems as if he is either enthralled or in terrible pain; I cannot tell.

"What's her name?"

"Barbara."

"Barbara," I repeat. Barbara, the flight attendant from Washington. January, the unemployed sales clerk from Roosevelt

Island. Barbara and Keith. January and Shazam. I imagine her life spread out before me in all its straightforward simplicity. Suddenly I feel how very unfair life can be, even cheating me out of a normal name. How different things might have been.

"January," Shazam says one last painful time.

"I don't want to move back to my parents' condo," I say.

Shazam is talking, saying things about "doing the best one can" and "counting one's blessings."

The traffic rushes outside and the saxophone next door squeaks on a sharp note. Something liquid and heavy has just made its home in my stomach. "Is this really how you want to go down in history?" I ask. What I really mean is fight for me. Fight for us. Say you're sorry and I'll forgive you.

But I don't say any of those things. The suddenness of our separation has anesthetized me. I feel neither regret nor longing, but I begin to sense that his name can no longer wound me. And right now, my deepest wish is for someone else to bear witness to that. And to what we look like at this moment, and to what we are wearing, and to our frailest gestures. I wish that someone, anyone, would walk in through the front door or drop down from the sky to find the two of us standing here, frozen, just like this.

Jack Cady

This is me and my aunt Helena, circa 1932. I look the same now as then, except with more hair and a beard. Aunt Helena is still alive and well, and nearing age ninety.

Jack Cady's most recently released novel, *Inagehi* (a Cherokee word that describes someone who lives alone in the wilderness), is set in North Carolina in 1957. Cady's body of work also includes *The Sons of Noah,* which won the World Fantasy Award for best single author story collection, and his earlier-written *Singleton* and *McDowell's Ghost.* Cady has published numerous stories and has won the Iowa Prize for Short Fiction, as well as the National Anthology Literary Award for short story.

Cady lives in Port Townsend, Washington, and has been adjunct professor at Pacific Lutheran University since 1987.

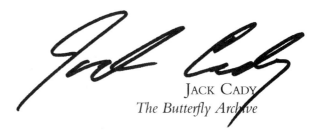

JACK CADY

The Butterfly Archive

I could have been little more than ten, and scarcely out of pinafores, when child-wandering led me to the Butterfly Archive. It was not in those days—or in these—actually known as such. It is called, when it is called at all, the Document Archive of Boston Towne, a curious building that nestles like a cellar above ground. The foundations are stone, but walls display centuries-old brick. The archive sits between brick row houses on one of the last sleepy streets of Boston. Brown leaves cluster in yew hedges that hide the building from the street. The leaves crackle and blow in autumnal bursts, even in spring and deep summer.

At age ten I did not yet recognize much difference between rich and poor, or men and women, but I did know myself as a New Englander. My father, a gentle man though stern, carried the name of Justice John Tilton. My mother was Prudence Glade Tilton, of the New Hampshire Glades. They each lived eighty-nine years, and tenderness dwelt between them, although it was tenderness a young girl only guessed. My parents were not cold, but they were New Englanders. Their hearts were carried elsewhere than on their sleeves.

Dark clouds scudded before a gale wind on that day of my childhood. As I wandered home from school, wind came

Glimmer Train Stories, Issue 11, Summer 1994

wrapped in the smells from storms at sea, or in nuances carried to eyes and nose from a waterfront where cloth and cordage and rum went aboard steamships bound to Australia or Zanzibar. If, in fact, I was ten, the year would have been 1924. Today I am seventy-nine.

Even to the eyes of a girl from Boston the building seemed threatening. In other, less solemn places, children might have been terrified. They would view barred windows and heavy oaken doors as having to do with jails or schools or prisons. They might see the copper roof, all green with tarnish, as proper shelter for the balding pates of judges. The normal child, being imaginative, is a first-class revolutionary against stuffiness; and normal children would imagine horrible crimes of law being perpetrated on free spirits.

I loitered a long while on that first day, waiting to see pirates dragged away in chains, or fallen women branded, or a hooded and black-robed inquisitor step through the doorway and pass by to enter a Duesenberg or Pierce-Arrow. The waiting produced nothing except the dry rattle of leaves and the movement of wind among ivy covering much of the old brick. In the hubbub of Boston town, this small corner sat in unperturbed silence.

I thought, while gazing at dusty windows which seemed to gaze back in studied indifference, that a shape moved within. Each time, my heart fluttered, not with terror, but with awe and question. At age ten, one is sometimes overwhelmed by the irrational power of the adult world. Children wonder how they will come to fit in such a world, because, of course, children do not believe they will change. They will only grow bigger.

I did grow and change. So did Boston town. But, in my heart of hearts, it was clear that I changed more than Boston. As I grew to adulthood and understanding, it became certain that Boston lies in the shackles of the past. It carries pride in its aristocracy, and pride because it is the seat of the American Revolution.

It does not deny, although it does not celebrate, its ancient flames of dogma. In Boston, 301 years ago, the Reverend Cotton Mather troubled over the use of "spectral evidence" as he fed the fires of the Salem witch trials. Nineteen people were hanged, two dogs were hanged, and Giles Corey was pressed to death as weights were piled on his chest.

In Boston, only 138 years ago, the best and the brightest of Boston collected money to support the abolitionist butcher John Brown. These facts, and many like them, seemed electric to the mind of a young woman, and they did not lose their voltage as that mind grew old.

When, at age thirteen and less timid, I once more approached the archive, it seemed that my comfortable world was about to crumble. My developing body suggested differences between men and women, and I was becoming a woman. The fact was alive with potential and dread. On more than one silly occasion, perhaps in a drawing room or at a piano concert, a man's eyes would engage mine for only a moment. The man would be handsome and well dressed and vibrant, and, being perhaps age twenty-five, would see me as only a schoolgirl. The schoolgirl, though, would begin to flutter and behave in a coy, schoolgirlish manner. Confusion made short shrift of Yankee common sense.

In those days, becoming a woman was thought to carry even greater responsibility than in the past. In 1920, with the passage of the Nineteenth Amendment to the Constitution, women won the vote. The whole world seemed in a whirl, times changing, while Boston town muttered testily against change.

I stood outside the archive as dry leaves fluttered. A horse-drawn ice wagon passed, the iceman huge and Irish and singing to his horse. Children followed the wagon, intent on grabbing small slivers of chipped ice when the man departed the wagon to make a delivery. Behind a dusty, sun-glazed window a figure moved. On a bold and impulsive notion, I stepped onto the sidewalk leading between yew hedges to the archive's door.

To a child, the woman who opened the door seemed old,

although she was not nearly as old as I am now. Wrinkles of smiles and wrinkles of sorrow webbed her face. Smoothly brushed hair fell nearly to her waist. Her hair was a shining cape of silver. Her dress fell to six inches above her ankles, a dress of dusty rose with small lace and small brocade. Her slippers were patent leather, of a kind made for dancing and not for a practical and workaday world. In my New England experience, no one moved so easily and with such quiet self-confidence. Her movements were as smooth as that cascade of beautiful hair. Her voice the same.

"This place has proved good shelter against most storms," she said pleasantly. "Even the storms of youth. Come in." She spoke so easily that I felt qualms. In my experience, new acquaintances were always taciturn. "This is where facts spin chrysalises," she told me. "Sometimes we hatch a butterfly."

She stepped back as I entered. She would prove wise in many ways, and one way dictated that the archive was best seen before being explained.

Overhead, timbers thick enough to be ships' keels supported that enormously heavy roof, and dusk dwelt between the timbers. The room lay like a vast, well-lighted cavern where shelves of books, journals, ships' logs, yellowed nautical charts, and court records covered brick walls and rose into gloom. Low bookshelves ranged across the enormous room and one might see over them so that, in a glance, it was possible to view an array of facts large enough to baffle all but the most experienced librarian. Yellow lamplight glowed in shadowed corners, and a wood stove at the farthest corner supplied heat that was not really needed at this time of year. A teakettle simmered, supplying water for tea and the needed amount of humidity. Oaken file cabinets ranked along one wall like soldiers at drill. One drawer in a central cabinet seemed to bulge a little.

"We're about to get a hatch," she said. "This one promises to be a bit dry." She walked toward the back of the room where tea things were kept in an old pie safe. Her desk held neatly arranged work, and I imagined it large enough to support a game of Ping-Pong. A small table was set for tea.

"My name is Amanda Mary Glade Tilton," I said, my voice shy. "I didn't mean to bother you."

"Mine is Elizabeth Smith," she said. "Just plain Elizabeth Smith, and almost nothing bothers me. Lies bother me; and, during the winters, one must dress very warmly in here. Except for those, I have no botherations."

On the wall behind her, and under glass, a Pine Tree flag from the American Revolution hung in faded green contrast to the faded red brick. I could almost hear fat explosions of black-powder cannon, feel the heeling of a small ship discharging a broadside. A variety of small arms hung on the long wall, together with tools and utensils and patchwork quilts, the quilts also under glass. Flat-faced portraits from the eighteenth century stared with stern, but not unfriendly, expressions. In fact, a portrait of a young woman with the unlikely name of Magdalen Beekman seemed nearly ready to smile and wink.

"And I am happy to say," Elizabeth continued, "that, because of my presence, few liars actually visit here. Liars, when pinioned on the collecting pin of facts, become disconcerted." She chuckled, as if sharing a private joke. "I have bagged more than my limit of such blatherskites." She glanced toward the file cabinet and the slightly bulging drawer. "Poor thing," she murmured, "to go to rest as a moth and emerge as a mayfly." She smiled at my confusion. "But you must tell me about yourself."

When you are thirteen and someone cares enough to ask about you, the conversation will surely turn toward hopes and dreams. I chattered and rambled that day. The cavernous room somehow seemed small and private because of the woman, or perhaps because of the tea things on the small table.

My dream in those days was to fly an airplane around the world. It seemed a sturdy dream then, and seems even more so now. At the time, Charles Lindbergh had not yet flown from Long Island to Paris, and would not for another three years. At the time, Amelia Earhart was still a teacher and social worker here in Massachusetts.

"An adventurer," Elizabeth muttered with approval. "It's no surprise. I might almost guess that adventure is borne in the bloodlines." She smiled at her statement. "Of course, we have no *facts* to prove such a guess."

The drawer of the filing cabinet trembled as if, within, a small but desperate battle flared. The drawer pushed open as much as half an inch.

"Facts are alive," Elizabeth said, "but unlike other living things they do not die. They metamorphose. Sometimes they lie dormant for centuries, but die they do not." She touched my hand, motioning me to accompany her.

We stood before the cabinet as a tiny, mud-colored beetle emerged to stand teetering on the edge of the drawer where it dried its wings. As the shell and wings dried, the insect took the sheen of old mahogany. It shone as a brilliant brown dot against the varnished oak cabinet. The archive filled with the sound of low rustling, and feelings of tranquility seemed warm as a featherbed. I did not understand Elizabeth's words, nor understand the value of a bug that might be squashed by the flick of a fingernail.

"Not a mayfly after all," she said. "Now it rises and reenters the world. This little fellow's value is that he will cause no change." We watched the beetle whir upward into gloom between the supporting timbers of the roof. "It's a drafty building," she told me. "He'll find a crack or crevice, then journey into the world."

She reached into the filing cabinet and pulled forth a folder that held a badly faded document, a sort of map.

"This is the scheme of an old water system," she explained. "Our ancestors had no metal pipes. They sawed logs down the middle, hollowed them out, then joined the pieces together. They sealed their wooden pipes with tar, then bound them with heavy hoops. Through the centuries the system decays. Just now, the last particle of that old system disappeared." Inside the folder, she wrote a precise note giving time and date, and which carried the comment: "returned to soil."

I could not fathom meaning from the event. At the same time, my practical Yankee assurance suffered. No one had prepared me to view a world of such implied power, or a world this intricate. My genuine fear was the fear of growing to adulthood. I desperately wished to remain a child.

"Facts are forces," Elizabeth murmured as she replaced the folder. "Forces of change, and forces of stability. Both are necessary, or the world gets knocked cattywampus." She looked upward where the fact had flown. "That little fellow has an important but quiet role. Our sparse New England soil lies slightly enriched. It waits for plow or steam shovel, or perhaps it waits to welcome a grave." Her words were stern, but her smile matched the patent-leather slippers which were made for dancing. "The whole business takes some getting used to."

Times changed. Change swept in great waves across the country. Change flooded across the craggy forehead of Boston town, and I, changing, met my share of liars.

Some liars arrived through the ether. The first radio station in our country was KDKA, founded in 1920. By 1927, radio liars across the country were in full cry. They called what they sold "ballyhoo." Today it is called "hype." The liars sold sensational news of murders and trials and seamy divorces. They sold stories of bold explorers (and some not so bold), as well as covert sex. As the blather increased, my mind did not retreat from adventure, but it often sought quiet and solitude.

I believed then, as I believe now, that to have a best friend and to be one is one of the great glories of life. During my thirteenth year, I returned time and again to the archive. No doubt I would have preferred a best friend of my own age, but in many ways Elizabeth seemed nearer to my age than did my schoolmates. Her cheerfulness, her kindness, and her dancing feet were compelled by a soul both happy and content. Although I witnessed the hatching of several facts, hearing and feeling their gauzy presence, Elizabeth did not mind that I remained more interested in dreams. A number of months passed before I actually encountered her anger and actually saw a wounded fact.

The fact fell from shadows between rafters on a snowy November day. Beyond the windows of the archive, giant elms lifted spectral branches into a storm-swept sky. Snow piled like mounded roads along the branches. In the streets no autos moved, and precious few horses. Elizabeth and I worked near the stove. We cataloged records of seventeenth-century sailing ships which had visited Barbados. Elizabeth's slippers were exchanged for patent-leather boots and wool stockings. Although styles dictated shorter skirts, I wore mine long. I clasped its folds between my ankles as we sat, a thick wool skirt that helped deny the chill.

The fact was a broken butterfly that might once have been a hopeful shade of green. Now it lay fluttering on the cold floor. Green faded nearly to white, and the butterfly secreted a tiny amount of clear fluid.

"It left here on strong wings," Elizabeth said, "and it returns flogged by lies. It is a weary creature, ready for rest." She knelt to cup the butterfly in the warmth of her hand. "It wishes to complete its cycle," she explained. "That's the reason for the release of sap." Her hands trembled.

My mind trembled. As Elizabeth carried the fact to a warm corner, I feared she would rage or perhaps launch into the air, flying into the stormy day, howling anger into the snow-burdened sky. I did not understand the meaning of the word "fury" until that day.

But she gently placed the butterfly in a box that contained dried grass, wood shavings, twigs, and thread. Then she moved toward a filing cabinet and withdrew a folder labeled "League of Nations." She made a note of date and time, and the comment: "This day, went to rest."

I feared her, but, because she was my friend, I also loved her. She now moved in a nearly aged manner, and I, at thirteen, had no wisdom to give, no comfort. Mystery dwelt all around us, and in this small event were enough forces to turn me from the ways of a child toward the struggle for adulthood.

Elizabeth stepped across the room to a heavily cross-referenced section of philosophy and religion. She pulled forth a folder and wrote: "On this date became current the 'Program of the N.S.D.A.P.' It contains the aims of a German political party called the Nazis."

I stood in amazement, not understanding yet knowing for the first time the awful power and weight of history.

"My reason tells me that I must not judge," Elizabeth said, her voice as tense as finely strung wire. "My good sense tells me not to tamper. There are times, though, when my heart would wish for a box made of Bessemer steel in which some facts could be locked for eternity."

My feelings were so confused that I nearly stuttered. I remember saying something about facts, wondering if the facts that lay around us went beyond Boston. Did this archive shelter all the facts in the world?

"It's complicated," she told me. "Physics says that for every action there is reaction. Much the same is true of facts. Facts string across centuries, knocking each other down like dominoes, and those dominoes are here. If, for example, Charles Martel had not defeated Abd al-Rahman at Tours in 732, this conversation might be held in Chinese."

At age thirteen, the abstraction was too difficult for me to grasp.

"If Israel Potter had not been at the Battle of Breed's Hill, the American Revolution might have failed. We might still bend our knee to an English king."

I almost understood, and was proud to know that the Battle of Bunker Hill had actually been fought on Breed's. In those days, children still studied history.

"But you are correct about Boston," Elizabeth told me. "Whenever anything good or bad rises in American history, look for its source in Boston. You may not find it there, but Boston is a very good place to start." Anger gradually drained from her voice as she taught me, while I did not even understand that she was teaching. "This town has birthed both darkness and light, but do not be fooled about darkness. Sometimes the blandness of evil is written on the whitest of vellum sheets. For centuries we have feared night and the darkness, then blamed others for that fear, but true night comes from within." She gently but firmly closed the drawer of the filing cabinet. "Do not visit here for a week," she said, and her voice was grim. "I do not want you to see the hatch from that drawer."

When I returned after a week of wishing to be with her, the

archive had suffered distress. Through nearly three centuries some cabinets had impressed the outlines of their bases in the pine floor. Now, here and there, tiny lines appeared showing the cabinets shifted by a quarter inch. Although the day twisted before the violent cold of northeast storm, the archive lay cloaked in the memory of heat. Elizabeth seemed not herself. Wrinkles of sadness around blue eyes exceeded wrinkles of happiness. Glowing silver hair had lost some luster.

"True witchery returns," she said. "Warlocks ride an ancient gale across the world."

"What hatched?"

"It was enormous, with black-and-red wings, and it was strong. The wings radiated heat and caused wind." She looked toward a row of cabinets holding sixteenth- and seventeenth-century documents. "A thousand cruel facts hatched with it. Every mindless fact of intolerance that ever spun to sleep awakened. A great cloud of facts." She looked at the backs of her hands where veins now stood prominent, hands that suddenly seemed old. She looked at my young face. "I hope I have not waited too long," she murmured, but she did not explain.

Nineteen twenty-eight whirled past, and much of 1929. Virginia Woolf published *Orlando*, Sigrid Undset won the Nobel for literature, and Georgia O'Keeffe painted *Nightwave*; the first Mickey Mouse cartoon appeared, and Benito Mussolini published his autobiography.

On Thursday, October twenty-fourth of 1929, when I was fifteen, a hatch began among bank records extending to the times of Alexander Hamilton and John Jay. Elizabeth watched the bulging file, and she watched me as she made a decision. "I feel my age," she said, "which means that you must grow strong quickly. This time I will not tell you to stay away."

On Tuesday, October twenty-ninth, the Great Depression sluggishly emerged to dry its wings. It was an enormous gray moth, of a size too large for an insect. The thick body hung over spindly legs like a flatiron perched on finishing nails. Wings beat as if the creature were tired, and would never cease to be tired. Wingbeats were whispers of sorrow as it rose into gray light between beams. Gray light flooded the archive, and even I felt old.

"There is howling and tearing in Europe," Elizabeth murmured, "and the Middle East trembles because Jews and Arabs are at war over the Wailing Wall. The Brits once more squabble with Afrikaners, and now this." She turned to me with the tenderness of a mother, but with the straightforward tones of a big sister. "Are you still an adventurer? Will you undertake the greatest adventure of all?"

I trusted her then, as I trust her spirit which still occupies this archive. By then it was obvious that one need not fly around the world to find adventure. Here, in this creaking archive, dwelt more power than could be generated by all the engines ever built.

She looked across the archive at rows of filing cabinets, at mementos of the past, at shelves of books rising like pillars of both fear and hope. "Who controls history, controls the future," she whispered. "Who serves history, perhaps serves the future. It's a Gordian problem, and it may be time to cut the knot."

When she looked at me she must have seen an earnest but unformed Yankee mind. She was courageous, because even now the very idea causes me to fear. "If we end up cutting knots," she said, "you'll have to know what you're doing."

The years of study began. They were years marking the world's anguish, but for me they were the happy years. We did not simply study the sweep and flow of history. We studied ways to bag a liar.

As the world heated up, the visits of liars to the archive became more frequent. While Germany began to rage, and while Stalin commenced killing twenty million of his own people, and while Chiang Kai-shek declared war on Japan, facts hatched like demons as liars congregated.

The liars were occasionally historians, but were more often genealogists. Some were the representatives of politicians. They came to the archive with briefcases and cordial smiles, and it was their intent to create an America that had never existed. They called for old records, but were selective about which records they read. A few of the liars were preachers, but the worst of all were the apostles of hatred.

And, of course, a few were not liars. It became increasingly important to know the difference.

"None of them can comprehend all of history," Elizabeth explained. "The ground rule is this: Are they here to seek understanding, or are they here to prove a point? If they're here to prove a point, be ruthless."

I watched her pinion many a liar. These were the days when hatemongers talked about "un-American Jewry."

"The facts are," Elizabeth whispered to one such rascal, "that Jews entered Georgia as early as the 1730s. They had synagogues in New York well before 1763. I suggest, sir, that Hebrew roots in this nation are deeper than those of your own family." She then smiled in a most friendly manner. "Review your conclusions and see if they can withstand public scrutiny. I will be obliged to refute you in the press."

It was an age of liars. Henry Ford lingered in the background as the hatemonger, Father Coughlin, priest of Royal Oak, stepped forth. By 1937, when I was twenty-three, anti-Semitism swept our nation and the world. Iraqi dictator Bakr Sidqi was assassinated, and Japanese planes sunk the U.S. gunboat *Panay*. Neville Chamberlain became prime minister of Britain, and Lord Halifax made a visit of appeasement to Hitler.

Across the world, other people fought back. Karen Horney published *The Neurotic Personality of Our Times* and Dos Passos published *U.S.A.* Marietta Blau measured cosmic radiation. Jose Ortega y Gasset published *On Love* and Picasso painted *Guernica*.

On September first, 1939, Hitler's armies drove into Poland, and the archive filled with wind. World War II was a monster with blood-reddened wings. The brick walls of the archive seemed about to push outward. Swarms of ebony flies and red bees circled into darkness between the beams. The stench of putrefaction followed the creature when solid oak doors blew open and it flapped into the night. Half of the file cases of history opened like screaming maws.

"We must fish or cut bait," Elizabeth said. "I suppose I always knew it would come to this." She turned to me. "You are very young."

By then, I was twenty-five. I responded by saying that I was getting older by the minute.

"It's dangerous to take a tuck in history," she told me. "The problems are moral and ethical. They are also practical."

It seemed to me that no nation could stop Hitler. That was practical.

"For good or ill," Elizabeth whispered, "this will be the great act of my life. It will exact a price." She stood before a neglected file in a remote corner.

"We are Bostonians," she said, "and Boston town is a prototype of America. It carries both justice and cruelty, but is ruled by stern New England conscience." She was resolute, but for a while she hesitated. "My conscience says to leave facts alone. My logic tells me to contain them. A third alternative is to fight facts with facts. Maybe that is honorable."

She reached into the file and drew forth a badly woven orange chrysalis. "Dormant since 1917 and not ready to hatch," she said. "God help us all."

A prematurely hatched fact is always awkward. Sometimes it is deformed. When Elizabeth cupped the fact in her hands and breathed it into life, the chrysalis split to reveal an ungainly creature that gnawed at its own legs as its wings dried. "It is cruelly pulled forth," Elizabeth whispered. "We can only hope it is strong enough. This creature is the spirit of the Russian people."

The fact rose on wings of green and gold and red. On June 22, 1941, German troops invaded Russia. They expected to encounter two hundred enemy divisions. They encountered more than three hundred and fifty.

Whether Elizabeth's action was correct or not, she was correct in knowing there would be a price. As the tyrant Hitler departed the world's stage, the tyrant Stalin stepped more firmly forth. In 1945, the war ended and I was thirty-one. Elizabeth was feeble through age and grave responsibility. She lived long enough to see the chrysalis of the League of Nations fly forth as the hopeful green hatch of the U.N.

"I shall become a cabbage moth," she whispered. "My soul will flutter above gardens, white-winged." By then, we were such friends that we could read many thoughts between us. "The Yankee disposition is judgmental," she told me. "It sometimes forces action." This was the only defense she ever offered, if it was a defense. "I never wanted power," she said. "I only wanted to serve. Plain Elizabeth Smith."

Her coffin lies in our sparse New England soil, but her spirit sometimes darts whitely from darkness between the beams. The commonly called cabbage moth is actually a butterfly, *Pieris rapae.* Elizabeth visited often during those years when I reluctantly carried the power to change history.

The 1950s roared onto the scene as liars congregated. Joe McCarthy descended into the madness of a witch hunt. Nixon made his Checkers speech. Nasser seized power in Egypt, and Dien Bien Phu was taken by Vietnamese communists. Television quacked its way into American homes, and hypesters learned that Khrushchev made hot copy. American troops ranged along the main line of resistance in Korea, and other Americans fought as well. Martin Luther King, Jr. stepped forward in Alabama. Arthur Miller published *The Crucible,* and once more appeared Esther Forbes's *A Mirror for Witches.*

Change pulsed as the nation became a world power. Marriage and divorce rates rose, as did birth rates, insanity, and suicide. Facts hatched in such great numbers that, for weeks together, I did not leave the sounds and flurryings of the archive. I became expert at bagging liars.

"Sir," I would say to some political opportunist who wished to build an America that never existed, "the first revolutionaries in our history were Anne Hutchinson, who came to Massachusetts in 1634, and Roger Williams in 1636. Neither was political, but each understood political hounds. Hounds such as yourself."

In 1962, when I was fifty-eight, a shy child of about ten stood before the archive on a chilly autumn day. Her school coat barely covered her knees, and her short, dark hair snugged tightly beneath a worn scarf. Her nose leaked because of the cold, and her cheeks were chapped and red. Her grandparents had obviously been members of the Italian immigration that came to Boston town in the early twentieth century. A girl from good stock; for immigrants, by definition, must be adventurers.

For the next three years, she occasionally returned to stand watching the archive. In those three years, files bulged and the hatch increased. By 1965, bizarre insects began to rise on psychedelic-colored wings. Turmoil lived between the darkened beams, and turmoil rocked the nation. Malcom X died of gunshot. Martin King marched from Selma to Montgomery. There were riots in Watts. However, Gambia became an independent state, and 1965 also marked the 750th anniversary of the Magna Carta.

On a December day winds blasted young trees, where once had stood mighty elms. I watched the girl walk timidly toward the great oak doors, and I opened one of them gently so she would not be frightened. "This place has proved good shelter against most storms," I said, and remembered Elizabeth. "You must warm yourself with a cup of tea."

"My name is Theresa Marie Lauricella," she said, "and I didn't mean to bother you."

"And mine is Amanda Tilton," I told her. "Plain Amanda Tilton. Not much bothers me."

She would become the child I never had, the daughter who might have been mine were it not that adventurers become absorbed in adventure. As she became comfortable at the archive, she combined a ready smile with dancing feet. In her practical manner, she viewed her adolescence as an inconvenience. She stood amazed and only a little frightened by night wings, but she stood absolutely thrilled at the emergence of true butterflies.

By 1968, when Theresa was sixteen, police rioted in Chicago, and Muriel Spark published *The Prime of Miss Jean Brodie.* The world lost writers. Died: Max Brod, Giovanni Guareschi, Fanny Hurst, Howard Lindsay, Salvatore Quasimodo, Conrad Richter, Upton Sinclair, Ruth St. Denis, John Steinbeck. American conscience gathered dust amidst the howling or it muttered questions while weeping over answers.

Theresa's own adventure began to incubate. It was my selfish hope that I would be allowed to remain a faithful keeper of facts. History might not force me into action.

It is true that through my career I occasionally breathed life into a fact, but it was always a fact that illuminated other facts. In the sixties, I breathed life into Eastern philosophy and religion. In the seventies, as musicianship declined, I would breathe life into the spirit of music. Sarah Caldwell would become conductor of the Metropolitan Opera. Musical groups ceased to hide behind their drummers. Leonard Bernstein gave the first performance at the Kennedy Arts Center. Reggae spread beyond Jamaica.

Theresa needed to learn our history of success and sorrow. She needed to take firm hold on the purity of her conscience. She had to learn how to bag a liar. More than all else, she had to learn the responsibility of power. About us lay facts for the taking and the twisting. We might launch them, or house them in boxes of Bessemer or finer steel.

In the years from '65 through '79, I progressed from age fifty-one to sixty-five, and felt my movements slow. Pope John Paul II was elected in '78. He visited America in '79. Theresa grew to womanhood and beauty. Her long hair reflected lights, swinging above dancing feet that moved like song across the old pine floor. It was her firm hand that began to faithfully record the hatch of that period: two million dead in Biafra, fuel shortages, Watergate, and the two hundredth coup and failed government of Bolivia. Stern wings beat harshly between the shadowed beams where, on the gravest occasions, also fluttered small white wings.

Wrinkles of laughter and sadness appeared around Theresa's eyes. The 1980s hatched. They emerged as a praying mantis, strong claws, and wings like wire. The creature's wings screeched as it rose into a sullen sky.

"You are still very young," I said, "yet you have worked hard."

"Getting older by the minute."

"There are computers. New ways of lying. There must be new ways to bag liars."

She loved a humorous situation. "We might be faithful to our trust if we practice on Mr. Kissinger."

As Babel grew the nation fell before forces of arrogance. Stupidity and greed are not new in human affairs, but now they were regarded as virtues. Saber rattling increased. The nation's symbol became a mouth, as the arms race hurried rapidly toward war.

I was deeply alarmed. We might put an end to a pandering president, or to a pornographer, but such facts would gnaw away at constitutional law. A change was needed, not only in the nation but in the world. I spent many a night grieving, many a night denying action.

Help arrived as spirits congregated. They came to me from where they fluttered above gardens. They dropped on silent wings from beneath the beams. Cabbage moths danced and circled in the air before my face. Whispers of conscience and whispers of resolution dwelt among them. Puritan voices they were, but some of them were tender. I understood that America is at its best when it is just.

These were the souls of the keepers of facts. This archive has now stood for three hundred and forty years. Through all that time, someone has held the reins of power. Elizabeth was not the first, and Theresa will not be the last.

They understood that a catalyst was needed. This was not a matter of minor change. This called for broad strokes of the pen across the pages of history.

When I reviewed the histories of all the nations of the world, attention gradually centered on Poland, and I felt no small amount of terror. That nation first appeared in the ninth century. It is a nation of idealism and destruction, of art and intolerance. It was the homeland of Copernicus and Conrad and Marie Curie, but also the home of the Vasa Dynasty.

Babel grew. Liars strutted while Afghanistan stumbled and the Middle East became a powder keg of terrorism. History pressed, and I controlled my mighty fear.

"This will be the great act of my life," I whispered to Theresa, "and there will be a price. When this bird flies, it will shriek."

The chrysalis holding the spirit of Poland was faded royal purple with broad streaks of white. It bulged with courage, but it also bulged with pogroms. I remembered my youth, the hatemongers of the thirties, the killing beliefs of the Axis.

"It is cruelly pulled forth," I whispered as I breathed it into life. "May God help it and all of us."

The hatching was tortuous. The chrysalis shuddered. It vibrated, resistant and thick-walled. When the creature emerged, it lay helpless, more like a baby than an insect. It finally rose on scarlet wings, a crippled butterfly beating unsteadily through the dusk. From files across the archive rose gnats and locusts, but also rose broad-winged creatures of color and beauty and hope.

History churned. Great forces were generated. Dominoes fell, and there is little more to say. The Berlin Wall is down. Europe once more enters turmoil. Old hatreds surface, and new tyrants stand ready to tread the stage. A new Nazi party demonstrates in

Germany, and, were he alive, not even the tyrant Tito could reunite Yugoslavia. I fear not for myself, but for Theresa. She need be strong. Unto her is bequeathed this fire.

And I? I never wished to take action. I only wished to serve, to be plain Amanda Tilton. My personal price is heavy. I never birthed a child, though I have helped form my dear Theresa. Facts, some of the butterflies, have warmed to life in my hands. Facts are my children. My personal price is the weight of responsibility that follows me to new adventure.

It is time to spin my own chrysalis, to draw my shroud closely and enter the gauze of history. I spin my metamorphosis toward our sparse New England soil. My shoulders slowly urge their way to wings.

My soul will become a cabbage moth. It will dance white above gardens which carry their own sense and symmetry of facts. I will serve as one of the keepers of the earth, one of the keepers without number.

Yet, I will visit here often in Theresa's early years. She is afloat in waters great and deep. Perhaps, as times become terribly troubled, Elizabeth and I will meet among the dusty beams of this archive, circling down from history. We will drop to glide about Theresa and brush our wings against the air before her face.

The Last Pages

JACK CADY

I started out to be a musician, not a writer. At about age fifteen, I really thought that the life most worth living was one spent behind a trumpet and in front of a swing band. As things fell out, I could never quite develop the circus-savagery of Harry James, the humor of Louis or of Muggsy Spanier, and would never catch the light touch of Ruby Braff. In other words, my horn was going to be only one more capable horn backing up the music of the spheres, and that was not going to be good enough.

Fifteen years later, at around age thirty, I undertook a venture into the music of language. Life improved immeasurably.

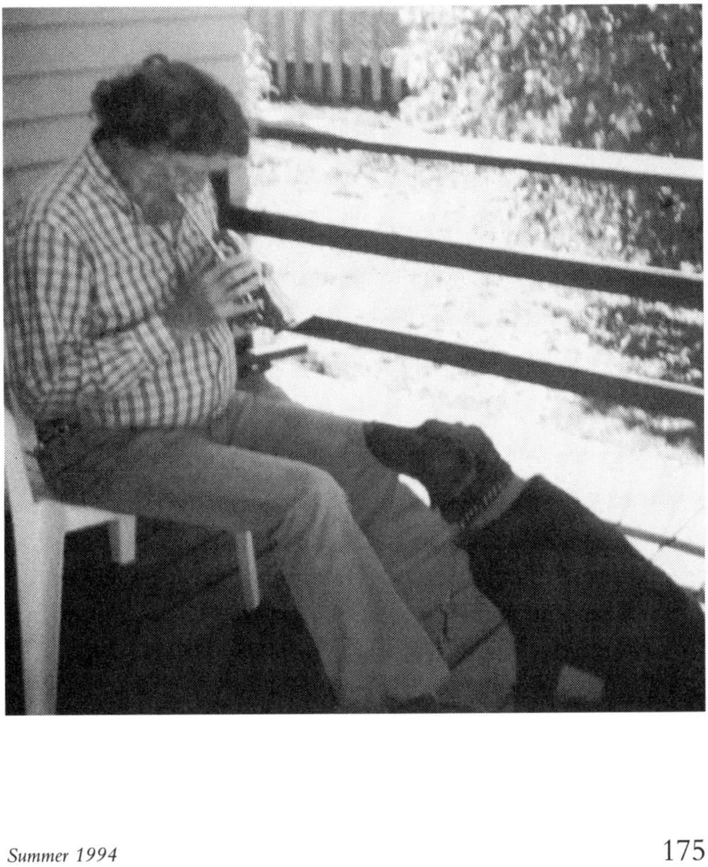

Richard Bausch

Generally, my work feels sporadic to me, in that I seldom keep to any fixed schedule, and I'm always feeling as if I should've worked longer or more arduously. Writing is a form of intense concentration, and so I don't feel time when I'm working. But it has never felt very organized or very efficient, and even so, it has always been one of the defining features of the day—that is, the kind of day it was often has to do with whether or not I've written, whether or not it went well, whether or not I felt like working or taking a little holiday from work (sometimes a really good day is a day when I haven't written)—and I have learned to accept it on its own terms and at whatever pace it seems to require. I never work less than two hours, and I have at times—especially toward the end of a novel, but occasionally on stories as well—worked as much as twelve to eighteen hours at a stretch. For instance, during the composition of the last parts of my novel *Rebel Powers*, I averaged twelve hours a day, taking three or four of those hours at night, usually.

I believe the work of a good writer undermines the tendency in a culture to see people only in terms of the groups they are part of—good writing presents the reality of others to us, and helps us see individuals where we might otherwise see only one form of stereotype or another. But beyond all that, one celebrates the simple human need for and delight in the story—from the earliest memory to the present. It has withstood every kind of concerted attack, and it will withstand all the depredations to come. That is what I depend on, and where my faith resides.

← This is a fair copy of how my daughter Maggie sees me. She's kind enough to give me more hair.

Robert Bausch

My son is an artist and writer. He's eight years old. Every day, he struggles with words and pictures. Sometimes he says, "I have writer's block." Sometimes he just curses and tears up paper. What gets thrown away or destroyed, he calls "mess ups." I am always with him in his struggles. Watching him work inspires me to do it. I tell him it never gets easier, although he might get luckier. He's going to be a writer all his life and, more than anything else, I hope he will have the kind of good fortune I have had.

Two of David's drawings. They are covers for two movies he's writing.

PATRICIA TRAXLER

A Musing on Faith and Luck

—from the novel *Earthly Luck*

More often than not, faith is sustained and passed along as family tradition. For the Irish, superstition is a kind of traditional faith—a folk faith. But not a blind faith, since that term implies faith without any basis, while for the Sweeneys and the O'Tooles, dreams, fortune-telling, and other modes commonly regarded as superstition are simply faith in what can be felt in all the cells of your skin, in the particles of dust that

float in random sunlight, in the turn of a page or a head at a propitious moment, in the Lotto numbers that "suddenly came to me for no good reason." And the nucleus which sits golden and eternal in the cytoplasm of faith is Luck. Luck. For the Sweeneys it has always been a religious virtue to have faith in *luck.* It's unthinkable, sacrilegious—not to mention bad luck—to ignore intuition, presentiment, hunch, or vision. Early on, a good Sweeney mother begins instilling in her children the ritual vehicles of intuition and superstition, along with an unshakable belief in luck.

No matter how often Norrie grumbled about the sixteen-million-to-one Lotto odds her mother was throwing money away on, Eileen Sweeney O'Toole would shush her daughter with admonitions to "have faith." *Maybe something good will happen*, Eileen intoned over the numbers each week like a priest over a wafer.

A call from her mother in the middle of the night was to say *Are you all right? I had a feeling* ... and always those calls came at a moment when Norrie was sitting up in the dark, cowering at a scary sound near her window, or looking up the six warning signs of cancer.

Norrie was never sure whether her mother was more holy woman or bookie.

FLOYD SKLOOT

I live two miles outside of Amity, Oregon, in a small, round house on a hilltop surrounded by fir and oak. Deer come by every day to eat what we have planted, even though the books tell us what we've planted is deer-proof. Skunks and raccoons come by, owls, bats, a cornucopia of songbirds, you name it. This is a long way from Brooklyn, New York. But it's where I have finally been able to write a novel about Myron and Faye, mismatch of the century, and the two children raised in their theater of operations. "The Fights" focuses on Myron in the years just before he married, and in particular on the love of his life, Sally O'Day, whom he did not marry.

The autobiographical sources of my fiction grow more mysterious to me as I get older. I don't know if there was ever a Sally O'Day in my father's life. He had a friend who was once a heavyweight boxer, but my father was not that friend's training partner or corner man. Nothing in "The Fights" happened in my father's life, as far as I know. Yet, the story feels terribly true to me about the violent man who died when I was fourteen. It has permitted me to grasp and say things about him and his life that I have always needed to grasp and say.

TIZIANA DI MARINA

"La Donna E Mobile" is dedicated to and was inspired by the life of my maternal grandmother, Elvira Aurelia Fiandra Patti.

Nonna Elvira died when I was seven years old, and the most important aspect of her death to me was the fact that I was not allowed to attend her funeral; as to be expected, this prohibition left me with little sense of closure, and I spent more than a decade dreaming about her as if she were still alive, dreaming that she was merely "hiding" behind tombstones in her graveyard, or dreaming that she had actually been resurrected from the dead.

"La Donna E Mobile" is only "true" in the sense that the emotions of the main characters are true; the way that I often write a story is to "catch" a certain emotion from the air and then make up the facts to go along with it.

In the case of Nonna, the emotion which I most "caught" from her, especially when I slept side by side with her, was the feeling of the bittersweetness of familial love.

This is not the story that Nonna would have written about herself.

This is a picture of my mother, Maria Rosaria Patti Lohnes. Since she is my primary link to the facts about Nonna's life, since she is an endless source of replenishment for me, I thought she deserved to be in the Last Pages.

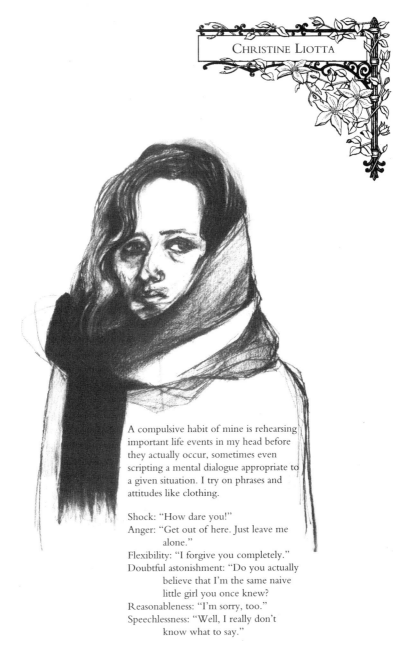

CHRISTINE LIOTTA

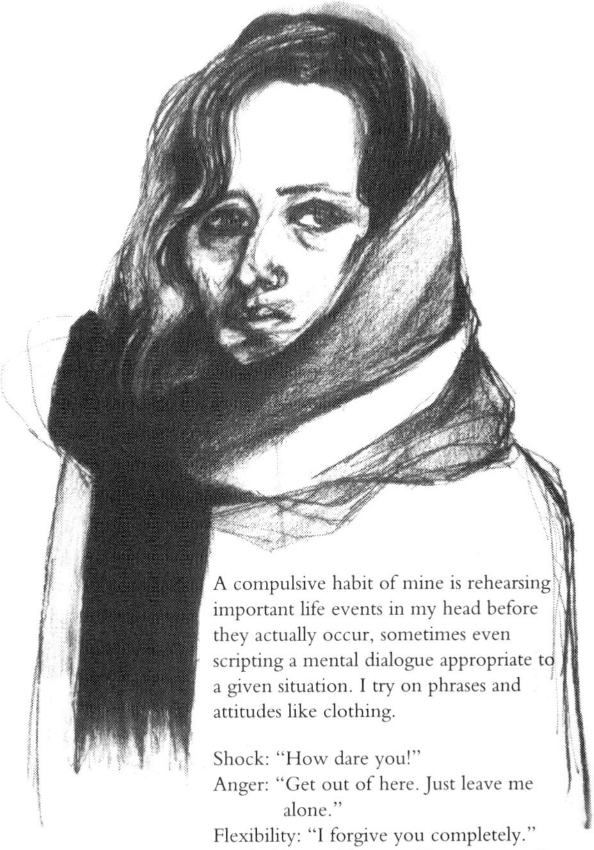

A compulsive habit of mine is rehearsing important life events in my head before they actually occur, sometimes even scripting a mental dialogue appropriate to a given situation. I try on phrases and attitudes like clothing.

Shock: "How dare you!"
Anger: "Get out of here. Just leave me alone."
Flexibility: "I forgive you completely."
Doubtful astonishment: "Do you actually believe that I'm the same naive little girl you once knew?
Reasonableness: "I'm sorry, too."
Speechlessness: "Well, I really don't know what to say."

One of the greatest qualities of being human is always knowing the perfect thing to say, only after the fact, when it's too late. In this sense I guess I've always longed for the sainthood of words.

STORIES GONE BY

Past issues are available for $11 each.

Joyce Thompson
Sports Cars
Abigail Thomas
Just Married 1960
Mary McGarry Morris
The Perfect Tenant
Wayne Johnson
On the Observation Car
R. Kevin Maler
Counterfeit
Marilyn Krysl
Extinct Species

WINTER 1992
Issue 1

Mary O'Dell
Yellow Pages
Anndee Hochman
Dark Is Not a Single Shade of Gray
Sigrid Nunez
Italics
Susan Burmeister
Steps to Goodness
Interviews with Patrick Tierney, street poet, and Gerard Byrne, painter, both from Dublin. Celia Wren on writers in South Africa.

Christopher Woods
Today, Quite Early
Abigail Thomas
Babysitting
Jack Cady
Tinker
Rosina Lippi-Green
Letters from Vienna
Gregory McNamee
The First Emperor
Corinne Demas Bliss
In the Perfect Privacy of His Own Mind
Lily King
Up in Ontario

SPRING 1992
Issue 2

Valerie Block
Java
Kathleen Tyau
How to Cook Rice
David Huddle
Reunion Joke
Stephen Dixon
The Stranded Man
Susan Burmeister
Second Tuesday
Interview with Portland artist Dennis Clemmens and interview with/article by Maina wa Kinyatti, a writer in exile.

Stan Rogal
Skin Deep
Daniel Wallace
My Old Vanity
Barbara Bechtold
Nushka
David Haynes
Busted
Marilyn Krysl
The Hiroshima Maiden
Elizabeth Inness-Brown
The Surgeon
Amy Selwyn
Mims

SUMMER 1992
Issue 3

Celia Wren
Liberation
Louis Gallo
Dead by Tuesday
Kyle Ann Bates
How It Is
Evelyn Sharenov
Magic Affinities
Susan Burmeister
Kites
Interviews with actress Vana O'Brien, and Siobhan Dowd, program director of PEN's Freedom-to-Write. Article by Siobhan Dowd, *Writer Detained: Maria Elena Cruz Varela.*

Janice Rosenberg
Chance of a Lifetime
Cathie Beck
Español
Terry Wolverton
A Whisper in the Veins
Joyce Thompson
First Day of School
Ed Weyhing
How Do You Know?
A. Manette Ansay
The Wallet
Jack Holland
The Yard

FALL 1992
Issue 4

Eileen McGuire
Inhale, Exhale
Mary Ellis
Wings
Stephen Dixon
Many Janes
Susan Burmeister
Pressing Tight
Interviews with writers Carolyn Chute and Stephen Dixon. Article by Siobban Dowd, *Writer Detained: Thiagarajah Selvanithy.*

Gary D. Wilson
What Happens Instead
Mary Ellis
Angel
Robert Abel
Prized Possessions
Lawson Fusao Inada
The Flower Girls
Lee Martin
Secrets
Sigrid Nunez
The Loneliest Feeling in the World

WINTER 1993
Issue 5

Elizabeth Judd
Mirrors to the Soul
James English
Goosewing
Susan J. Alenick
Chips and Whetstones
Susan Burmeister
Man across the Aisle
Interviews with writers William Styron and Joyce Thompson. Article by Siobhan Dowd, *Writer Detained: Gustavo Guzman.*

STORIES GONE BY

Floyd Skloot
The Royal Family
Marina Harris
Skin Tailoring
Joyce Thompson
Who Lives in the Basement
Libby Schmais
Losses
Louis Gallo
And the Greatest of These
Daniel Gabriel
In The House of Mr. Poo
Stephen Dixon
Hand

SPRING 1993
Issue 6

Peter Gordon
The Net
Danit Brown
Breathing
Wayne Karlin
Dov's Toes
Susan Burmeister
When Lila Comes Home
Interview with writer Anne Rice and *Glimmer Train* illustrator, Jon Leon.
Article by Siobhan Dowd, *Writer Detained: Mansur Muhammad Ahmad Rajih.*

Liz Szabla
Dearborn
Joyce Thompson
First Out
Joyce Carol Oates
The Missing Person
Kiran Kaur Saini
A Girl Like Elsie
Roxana Robinson
Sleepover
Richard Bausch
The Natural Effects of Divorce

SUMMER 1993
Issue 7

Stewart David Ikeda
Roughie
Katherine Min
Objects
Stephen Dixon
Interstate 3, Paragraph 2
Susan Burmeister
The Two-Step
Interviews with writer Doris Lessing and blues singer Linda Hornbuckle.
Article by Siobhan Dowd, *Writer Detained: Ren Wanding.*

Daniel Wallace
The Main Thing
Ursula Hegi
Blue Edge of the Continent
Frances Kuffel
Gulf Wars
Ed Weyhing
Empty Gesture

FALL 1993
Issue 8

Anatoly Kurchatkin
Home
Michael Dorris
Qiana
Interviews with writers Jonathan Raban and Charles Johnson.
Article by Siobhan Dowd, *Writer Detained: Yndamiro Restano Diaz.*

Louise Erdrich
Resurrection
Abigail Thomas
So Far, So Good
Mary McGarry Morris
My Father's Boat
Hester Kaplan
Spiral
Lex Williford
Macauley's Thumb

WINTER 1994
Issue 9

Charles Baxter
Reincarnation
Peter Parsons
Where Do We Go from Here?
Interviews with writers Charles Baxter and Bob Shacochis.
Article by Siobhan Dowd, *Writer Detained: Hwang Suk-yong.*

Ellen Gilchrist
A Statue of Aphrodite
Rosina Lippi-Green
Katy-Marie, Austria 1943
Kent Gardien
Springtime Lunchtime
Robert A. Abel
X
Thomas E. Kennedy
Bonner's Women

SPRING 1994
Issue 10

Ann Beattie
Solitude
Randolph Thomas
Chronology
Lex Williford
Hoot's Last Bubble Bath
Interviews with writers Mary McGarry Morris and Kathleen Tyau.
Article by Siobhan Dowd, *Silenced Voice: Taslima Nasrin.*

What a marvelous convergence!

Leni calls me for advice. All the time. It could be three in the morning, maybe on a Tuesday, a workday, and the phone will ring. "Hello," I'll say. "It's me," Leni will announce, and then he'll go straight into it, whatever it is.

from "Leni Calls Me for Advice" by Jiri Kajane

With their white helmets, plastic goggles, Lycra bodysuits, and awkward postures hunched over the expensive racing bikes, and the strident whirring of their tires, they resembled some sort of large, swift insects—locusts perhaps.

from "The Entrepreneurs" by Tony Eprile

"No, thanks just the same, Melinda. They say there's as much caffeine in a tea leaf as a coffee bean. You'll note back in history it wasn't until Marco Polo opened the tea routes that Europe became dangerous. All that caffeine."

from "Yesterday after the Storm" by William Luvaas

And then he remembered the feet. They had golden feet. Were there gowns? He hadn't noticed gowns, only the tight, determined faces and small buttery feet. Their arms had stretched out and caught the tree, held it there just long enough. Millie would claim he was having a low-sugar fit, that he had eaten too little breakfast, or too much.

from "Golden Feet" by Elizabeth Logan Harris

Plus the winning story of our first semiannual Short-Story Award for New Writers!